Damaged Goods

Also by Debbi Mack

Damaged Goods

An Erica Jensen Mystery

Debbi Mack

Renegade Press

Savage, MD

Renegade Press
P.O. Box 156
Savage, MD

Library of Congress Cataloging-in-Publication Data
Damaged Goods by Debbi Mack
ISBN: 978-1-7341094-1-2
Library of Congress Control Number: 2020902849

DEDICATION

This book is dedicated to my husband and family with love and gratitude.

PROLOGUE

Afghanistan, November 2011

Ten minutes. It was only supposed to take ten minutes to reach our ride home.

Perkins drove. I rode in the vehicle commander's seat. An electric jolt ran up my spine as our allegedly mine-resistant vehicle bounced down the dusty road. If you could dignify the narrow strip of packed sand as such. The same relentless beige as its surroundings.

Corporal Perkins spat out an oath behind a keffiyeh tied across his nose and mouth. My face was also half-encased with cloth. The idea was to keep from choking on the cloud of sand and dust that swirled around us. But the grit managed to work its way behind our makeshift filters. My face itched with the stuff. Under the desert sun, I squinted behind the dark Eyepro strapped tight to my head. The goggles reduced the glare and kept the dust from blinding me.

Perkins' oath was swallowed up by the roar of the vehicle and the howling wind.

"Copy that," I shouted, although he could no better hear me than I could hear him. I gripped my M16A4 rifle a little tighter as I scanned the surroundings.

Perkins, a red-haired, freckle-faced 20-year-old, said something else. I motioned for a restatement, pointing to my ears and shaking my head. The muffled response was, "Erica, are … okay?"

Perkins was one of the good guys. He saw and acknowledged that women were a military asset. Women have aided combat troops for years—unofficially, of course—as far back as the American Revolution. Back in '04 or '05, the Marines led the way for women to become more officially involved. When I deployed, they assigned me to the Female Engagement Teams or FETs. This was a highly select group of women who performed valuable back-up to the ground troops and intel-gathering duties. The types of jobs men couldn't perform because of cultural niceties.

"Erica?" Perkins' voice pierced my thoughts like a knife.

He'd been asking after my health. I had sustained a concussion while riding at the tail end of a convoy. My concentration still suffered, even after spending weeks in a hospital. I tried to conjure a response, but the wind seemed to blow thoughts straight out of my head. "I'm fine," I yelled.

I checked my watch. Seven minutes to go.

Perkins was hell-bent on returning to his hometown in Nebraska or Kansas or some other big-ass state full of fields, small towns, and DQs. I think his family raised hogs. Me, I could think of no other place to go except the DC suburbs, where I had lived all 20 years of my life. With the exception of the last two, which I'd spent in Afghanistan.

Perkins had an advantage over me, in that he had a family he wanted to go home to. My parents thought I was insane to join the Marines. Maybe they were right, but their alternative was for me to go to college and marry well. Not my idea of a life plan.

I'd miss the people here, my comrades in arms and the ones we'd served. Even men who had greeted the FET as skeptics were eventually won over by our ability to connect with the locals, gather intel, and watch the men's backs. Despite everything, I actually felt like we were a force for good. When we weren't being blown to bits.

I wouldn't miss the Vietnam War–era equipment the Army had abused and foisted on us, the whipping, grit-filled wind, the inedible food, scorching summer temps, and freezing nights, and especially playing target for madmen.

I scanned the nearby area for signs of movement as the barren desert wasteland stretched for miles around us. My watch indicated five minutes until we reached our ticket out of here.

Then, clear as a bell, I heard Perkins say, "First thing I do when I get home is have a cheeseburger. And a bottle of beer."

As I opened my mouth to reply, I felt a sudden blast. Day turned into night. *Is this death?* I thought, before slipping into the void.

CHAPTER ONE

I jerked awake in my bed, drenched in sweat. Eight years had passed and I still had the dream. I was alive, Perkins wasn't.

The room was a dark blur. My head was throbbing, and I blinked rapidly to clear my vision, but that didn't work. I stared at the bedside clock and forced the numbers into focus. 0430 hours.

I flopped back on the bed and stared at the ceiling. Was another hour of sleep really worth it? Did I even want to go back to sleep?

"Oh, what the hell," I grumbled. I turned off the alarm and threw the covers aside before slowly swinging my feet to the floor. I had an important meeting that morning and didn't want to be late.

I peeled off my sleep shirt and trudged into the bathroom for a warm shower, hoping it would relax me and wash off remnants of the dream. After a vigorous towel down, I put on my robe and went to the kitchen to brew some strong coffee. The paper wouldn't be delivered for another hour. I like reading an actual print newspaper. Yeah, I'm weird that way.

After filling my coffee mug to the brim, I dry-swallowed two Advil and sipped the hot brew. A poor substitute for the painkillers I was forced to quit, as part of my court-ordered therapy. My aching brain cried out for just one tablet from my hidden stash of leftover Oxy. Excuses and reality bounced back and forth in my head. *But it's an emergency* . . . Focus, I thought.

I puttered around the kitchen, making a simple breakfast of English muffins slathered in butter and Marmite (a salty British condiment you either love or hate). After washing the few dishes and utensils, I did a 10-minute meditation to prep for the day followed by yoga stretches to strengthen my back and get my head right. As I went through my ritual, I steeled myself for a meeting with a new client—a multi-millionaire no less.

I'm not what you'd call a real private eye. My return from Afghanistan was hardly auspicious. I came back a physical and mental wreck, thanks in part to outmoded or inappropriate gear and vehicles. The ill-fitting heavy armor had worn my spine down something fierce. As for the explosions I survived before leaving the country, let's just say noises as threatening as a slamming door made me as jumpy as a cat in a dogs-only kennel. Back then, scenes from the war played in my head like a movie on a continuous loop. Between that and my aching back, I couldn't sit still for even ten minutes.

A few years of physical and occupational therapy helped me manage the worst of the war's toll on my body. As for the mental aspects, I was still in recovery. Probably for the rest of my days.

I found office work absolutely unbearable. Office politics aside, my coworkers seemed to bitch nonstop about tiny problems—which drove me nuts.

I ended up working as a freelance researcher by developing the kind of computer skills needed to track down debtors— deadbeat dads, deadbeat moms, deadbeats of all stripes. I even did a little repo work, such work as I could get. That plus pain pills and therapy—court-ordered and otherwise—kept me afloat.

The most recent call for my services came right out of the blue—on a Sunday no less. I had been referred to Stuart Blaine by one of my previous clients. All my clients are by referral. Frankly, most of them aren't in a position to pay the freight for a legitimate private eye.

It's an unfortunate fact of life that one can't obtain a private investigator's license in Maryland if one is addicted to narcotics. According to the VA and the judicial system, I was such an addict. Advil, therapy, and yoga notwithstanding.

The fact that Blaine made more than enough money as a real estate developer should have raised at least one red flag. But he claimed it was an emergency and wanted to meet me as soon as possible. My calendar wasn't exactly overflowing with multi-millionaire clients, so we arranged to meet the following morning.

Before leaving home, I double-checked my appearance. My dark blue suit wasn't Nordstrom, but it placed well above Goodwill. I tugged at the jacket and fiddled with tights so sheer, they might as well have been pantyhose. I loathed dressing up to impress some big shot, but I needed the money. What a way to start a Monday. Hopefully, a few hours in this getup would be worth the inconvenience.

φφφ

At 0900 sharp, I stood at the doorstep of a small palace in upper Montgomery County, Maryland. Me in my monkey suit, looking the part of a down-and-out relative, outside a mini-manse, totally out of my element. But money is money.

Stuart Blaine's assistant answered when I rang the doorbell and asked me to wait in the foyer. I waited. The sound of a hushed discussion drifted down the stairs and made my skin crawl—as if there were ghosts up there. Then footsteps. Blaine appeared, descending the grand staircase curving from the second floor.

Blaine couldn't have been taller than four foot ten, more than a half-foot shorter than me. In his mid-fifties, he was a stick figure with pasty skin and green eyes made huge by the Coke bottle lenses in his glasses. Even with the wealth of a modern-day Midas, he sported cheap eyewear. Maybe penny-pinching was the secret of his success. He wore jeans and a plaid flannel work shirt that had worked so hard, its sleeves fell off. Blaine's scrawny upper arms bore an elaborate blue and purple skull-and-flowers tattoo. Here I was, the hired help, dressed to the nines, while Blaine looked like an overage slacker. The vibes from this scene were totally unnerving.

He extended a hand as he approached. "Thanks for coming to see me, Ms. Jensen."

"It's good to meet you, Mr. Blaine." As we shook, he held onto my hand, as if for dear life.

"Please . . . call me Stu."

"Yes, sir. Stu. I'm Erica."

Blaine led me through an area decorated in classic Ethan Allan. "This is the family room," he said over his shoulder. "Not my style, but it'll do until I can update the look."

"Here's the kitchen." He waved toward the small room. "It needs to be expanded and upgraded." Blaine's compulsion to provide these explanations made me wonder if he mistook me for an interior decorator. We took a short hall to a room lined with bookshelves. A sleek Danish modern desk sat near the picture window.

I quickly scanned the heavy dark wood bookshelves, which held a mix of hardcovers and paperbacks, informal popular titles.

"This is the library." Blaine stopped and swept his hand in a sideways arc. *No shit.*

"Please have a seat." He nodded toward a guest chair. Apparently, the house tour was over, so we could get down to business.

Blaine dropped into his high-backed leather chair, and judging from his not being completely dwarfed by it, I could've sworn the tiny man was using a booster seat. He propped his elbows on the desk and gazed at me over steepled fingers. "My daughter is missing," Blaine said without preamble. "I'm willing to pay whatever you ask to find her."

Odd. During our phone call, Blaine had given another reason for hiring me.

"You told me your former partner may have embezzled from you," I said. "Now you tell me your daughter is missing. Have you called the cops to report her missing?" He looked confused, so I added, "How old is your daughter?"

"She's twenty-two, single, and going to art school in Baltimore. She hangs around with losers who borrow money and party all night." Blaine raised a hand, palm forward, silencing me. "I also have the problem I mentioned on the phone, but that's a separate issue."

Really? Despite the money I stood to earn, this wasn't the best start to a potential business relationship.

"Your daughter isn't a minor, so she can go where she wants," I said.

Blaine glared at me. "Did you not hear me? She's hanging out with a bad crowd. I haven't been able to reach her, and that's unusual. I'm worried."

You want to control her life. Tell her who and what to be. Is it any wonder she's dropped off your radar? Too much like my own parents.

I took a breath before speaking. "Let's take things one at a time," I suggested. "When did you last hear from your daughter?"

"Thursday night."

Four days ago.

"You can file a missing persons report any time," I said.

He frowned. "No cops. That's why I need you."

I could already guess his reasons, but I had to ask. "Why not call the police?"

He grimaced. "Young lady, do you read the papers? Or do you just surf the Web for funny cat photos and weird celebrity news?"

I let that condescending remark slide. Blaine seemed like the kind of guy who confuses taunting with being assertive. Besides, even though I had just turned thirty, I've been told I look seventeen, which doesn't help.

"I know who you are," I said in an even tone. "I know you were released from prison last year."

"Then you should understand why I would rather not have the police involved in my personal business."

I nodded. Being a convicted drug dealer must complicate one's life. *Cry me a river.*

"Assuming I agree to find her, any guesses about where your daughter may have gone?"

"I have no idea." A vertical line creased the space between his brows. "She could be anywhere."

Blaine had no clues about his daughter? Not exactly Father of the Year material. "So . . . she's never expressed a desire to leave the area?"

He waved a hand. "She's mentioned wanting to see the Southwest, but I doubt that she actually went there."

"How can you be sure?"

"She's determined to graduate from the Maryland Institute College of Art and has already wasted a lot of money on classes there."

"You don't pay her educational expenses?"

"I told her if she insisted on going to art school, it would be on her own dime." Blaine pursed his lips. "She can't tap her trust fund, except for emergencies. Art school doesn't qualify."

Asshole, I thought. I resisted the urge to point that out. "How about her friends? Have you tried talking to them?"

"I have no contact with the people she hangs with now." A wistful tone crept into his voice. "Her best friend in high school was Katie Saunders. I don't know if they've stayed in touch."

"How about guys? Any special ones in her life?"

"She sees so many boys I can't keep track." The wistfulness was gone and his tone was flat.

Not helpful. Maybe Katie would know more.

I pressed on. "What about social media? Is she on Facebook or Twitter?"

Blaine scowled. "I don't post or tweet or snaptweet or whatever they're doing these days. I leave the social media work to my partner." He waved a hand, as if swatting flies. "My daughter works at a coffee shop near the school. Cafe Latte or some such. I can't recall her saying anything unusual or dropping any hints that would help you find her."

"How do you know she's missing? Have you been to her home?"

Blaine's expression turned stiff, his lips pressed thin. "We usually talk every Friday or Saturday, except for this past weekend."

I pondered the non-answer. Was he deliberately evasive or simply obtuse?

"Does she usually call you or vice versa?" I asked. When faced with verbal ninja moves, respond in kind.

"I always call. She usually answers or gets back to me."

"What happened over the weekend?"

"I left a message." Blaine brushed non-existent dust off the arm of his chair. "Haven't heard a thing."

"So did you go to her place?" *Patience.*

Blaine's expression crumpled. "I don't know where she lives," he admitted.

I had read that Blaine was divorced, so the next question would be tougher.

"What about her mother?"

"What about her?" His tone invoked the sound of thunder.

"Does she have a good relationship with her mother?"

Blaine shook his head like a wet dog. "I don't know. We don't talk about her. If you knew my ex, you'd understand why."

What a guy.

"I'll need to talk to her mother. Just in case." This interview was turning out to be as much fun as a DIY root canal.

Blaine released a breath with Arctic warmth. "Fine," he said, and offered up his ex-wife's email, phone, and address in California as though it were a state secret.

When I asked about other close relatives, Blaine claimed there were none.

"Here's what I'll do," I said. "I'll spend three hours looking for her. I'll check with her friends and contacts around school and work. Do some online research. If I don't get any leads, I'll check back with you. But to be honest, any further work may be a waste of your money and my time."

"Now, see here—"

I leaned forward and glared at him. "No, listen. If her disappearance is . . . " my voice trailed off, but I resumed speaking in a lower tone, " . . . due to foul play, the police must

get involved. Given the unusual nature of my services, I don't
want to tread on official toes. Understand?"

His expression turned sullen, but he nodded.

"Now," I continued. "About the missing partner and money.
I can understand why you'd wish to keep this quiet and avoid
official interference with your business. I'll need more details—
your partner's name, the amount missing, and any information
that could help me find him and the money."

Blaine launched into a story about how he and his partner,
Slava Kandinsky, had knocked heads over marketing,
reinvestment in the business, and other matters. Kandinsky had
kept the books and was a spender. Blaine wanted to rein in
extravagant purchases and focus on reinvesting to shore up the
basics. He claimed that ten grand was unaccounted for. I
nodded and took notes.

"And the name of your business?" I asked.

"B & K Developers, LLC."

That much I knew from reading the papers.

"When did you last see him?" I asked.

He squinted and pinched his chin between thumb and
forefinger. "Last Wednesday, maybe. Yeah, that was it. He called
me on Thursday, claiming he was sick. I didn't notice the
discrepancy in our records until Friday. And I've been unable to
reach him at home or on his cell."

Sucks when no one returns your calls. I paused to think of a good
way to ask the next question. "How well does Kandinsky know
your daughter?"

He paled a bit, but answered with authority. "Far as I know,
they've never met."

Right. Keep telling yourself that.

"One more thing," I said. "It'll save me a lot of time if you
tell me your daughter's name."

He smiled and shook his head. "What was I thinking? Her name's Melissa. Her full name is Melissa Anne Blaine."

I jotted down the name and very much wondered what he was thinking.

CHAPTER TWO

Before I left Blaine's palace, he dredged up a photo of Melissa. It was her high school senior photo, so she might have dyed her hair or who-knows-what in the five years since she graduated. In the photo, her mousy-brown locks were brushed back from a perfect oval face that featured full lips and her father's green eyes.

Blaine also gave me copies of articles about B & K Developers, including one with a full-color photo of Blaine and Slava Kandinsky sitting side-by-side. Kandinsky had longer legs, knees sticking out at awkward angles compared to his shorter partner's. He had a swarthy complexion and eyes that gleamed like wet tar.

I left the house and crossed a driveway that led to a three-car garage, slipped into my blue Fiesta, and fired it up. I lowered the windows to let in the warm, early September breeze. Then I drove to the local library, took my file and laptop inside, and started to put my thoughts on paper while they were still fresh.

When I start a case, I like to create a flowchart. In this case, I had to find two people who may or may not have known each other. So I turned to a blank page in my notebook. Yes, I use paper and pencil for this stuff. I refuse to go all digital.

I penciled in the name "Melissa Anne Blaine" on the right side, making an oval around it. Under her name, I wrote "MICA", the acronym for the art school, pronounced "mike-ah." On the left, I wrote "Slava Kandinsky" and drew a rectangle around that, then added the few additional names I'd squeezed out of Blaine. I put my client's name at the top of the page and underlined it, then drew arrows between that and each of the others, noting the relationships along the lines.

With the preliminaries out of the way, I turned on the laptop and scoped out Melissa's last-known address and social media presence. Nothing. Not finding her on Facebook wasn't surprising, since teens and young adults are apparently fleeing the site. However, Melissa's friend Katie Saunders was there and was identified as a graduate of Damascus High School. I next turned to Instagram—the logical place for a young artist. And Pinterest. But there was no sign of Melissa on either one.

I needed to delve deeper by using a subscription database—one of the few I can afford. I avoid using those outside my home, because I'm concerned about wi-fi security (or lack thereof). The downside is that some of these databases are often weeks or months out of date. I would have to rely on my threadbare people skills to gather the most recent intel. I set my sights on Katie Saunders first.

I looked online for all the Saunders listed in the Damascus, Maryland, area. There were only five—Damascus isn't exactly a huge metropolis. After jotting down the numbers and addresses, I left the library, returned to my car, and dug my cell phone out of my shoulder bag.

I punched in the first number, and someone of indeterminate gender rasped a greeting.

"Hi," I said. "Is Katie there?"

"Who? Kaley?"

"No. Katie."

"Either way, you've got the wrong number." I heard a click, and that was that.

I kept going and hit pay dirt on the fourth try. A woman who sounded like someone's grandmother answered. When I asked for Katie, she said, "She's away at college, dear."

"Would you mind if I got her number, ma'am?" I chirped. "I'm putting together a contact list for the next high school reunion." I figured the lie would protect Stuart Blaine.

"Well, I don't know . . . I'll need to ask her mother."

"Is she there?" I pressed. "Can I talk to her?"

"She's out, but she should be back soon."

"How about if I check back in half an hour?"

"She might be back by then, although you may want to wait an hour, just to be sure."

"Awesome," I gushed. We exchanged brief farewells and hung up.

I had no intention of calling in an hour; I would go to the house instead.

I started the car and headed toward a shopping center I had noticed on the way to see Blaine. There was just enough time to grab a sandwich from the deli before stopping by the Saunders' house.

I bought a Reuben on pumpernickel, which I wolfed down while I scanned my notes and planned my general strategy. I would need to visit the art school, of course, and I could swing by the coffee shop while I was there. And as for Mr. Kandinsky, I would deal with him in good time.

As I ate and reviewed notes, I stayed alert as always to my surroundings. Not that I expected anyone to attack me here, but old habits die hard. Fortunately, this wasn't the bar where some drunk had tried to feel me up. I hadn't expected that, either.

And he hadn't anticipated my fist connecting with his nose. Good thing I hadn't connected squarely. I could have smashed his nose right into his brain.

That kind of behavior lands you in court. Which leads to court-ordered anger management therapy. Which extends into talk therapy, ad infinitum. So many words, so little progress.

I finished eating, did the minimal amount of cleanup expected of good citizens, and left.

Katie Saunders' house was tucked behind a stand of trees at the end of a long driveway. The architect must have been a fan of Frank Lloyd Wright's late period work. The house had a post-post-modern design—all sharp angles and big windows. The property slanted downhill in back, and a porch surrounded the house, cantilevered over the hill by large beams. The driveway ended in a circle, making it easy to turn around. How considerate.

The sound of birds singing floated up from the woods behind the house. I left the car next to a bed of yellow and orange marigolds and walked up to the front door. After I rang the doorbell, I could hear a set of chimes echoing faintly from somewhere inside.

The door was opened by a woman who looked too young to be the mother of a college student. She was wearing khaki shorts, an oversized green polo shirt, and glasses with blue rectangular frames. Her blonde hair was tied back into a low short ponytail, and her cheekbones were high and sculpted.

"Our housekeeper says you're looking for Katie?" she said, before I could get a word out.

"Yes, ma'am. I'm Erica Jensen." I extended my hand, but the woman didn't shake it.

"And why do you need to talk to her?" Her face was expressionless, but her voice had an edge.

"I'm with the reunion committee. We're updating our contact list. Are you Katie's mother?"

The woman's eyes widened. "Good god, no! I'm her older sister. Mom asked me to take care of this." She flapped a hand, as if drying her nails.

"Look," I said, adopting an easygoing tone. "I just want to be able to reach Katie, when we start planning the big reunion."

"Well." The word hung between us. She scrutinized me for a long moment. "Which high school did you say this was for?"

"Damascus," I said. Good thing I had checked Facebook. "I didn't catch your name."

She crossed her arms, as if to hold the information to her bosom. "I didn't pitch it. So, why do you really need to reach Katie?"

This was going downhill fast. I could either come clean or punch this woman in the face, which wouldn't help my cause.

"Why do you ask that?" I said.

The woman smirked. "You could find that information easily if you were really on the reunion committee."

This game was already getting tiresome. "Look," I said. "My name is Erica Jensen and I'm looking for Melissa Blaine. She's missing and may be in trouble." Okay, that was pushing things. But my intentions were good. "I understand she and Katie were friends, and I was hoping Katie could help me find her."

I fished out my business card with my name, contact information, and the words "Research Service" underneath.

She glanced at the card. "Research service. Is that what they're calling private eyes these days?"

"I don't normally handle missing persons cases." My patience was running thin. "Can you help me or not?"

"Sorry, but no." She tucked the card in her pocket. At least she hadn't thrown it in my face.

As she closed the door, I said, "Is there a reason you won't help me find Melissa?"

In response, she simply smiled. Then, the door thudded shut.

CHAPTER THREE

As I drove home, I mulled over the odd behavior of Katie's sister. I understand why people want to be left alone, but looking up a number for me? To help find a missing person? Seriously?

I pushed aside any more thinking about Katie's sister and her 'tude. It was weird, but that was her problem, not mine. I sped south down New Hampshire Avenue, turned onto Randolph Road, then snaked through a series of backstreets toward a side road off Georgia Avenue in Wheaton, to my apartment-office.

I had managed to find a studio apartment I could barely afford at the Heights, a building rehabbed from a sixties-era mid-rise into a gleaming high-rise tower. It was a short walk to the Metro Red Line. Not to mention all sorts of fancy new stores and the arts district. All part of the suburban renewal effort of the past few decades.

I pulled into the garage and parked as close to the entrance as possible. I grabbed my notes as I left the car and walked up the two flights to my place. The apartment was just big enough to suit my needs. A short hall led past the bathroom on the right and opened into my living room-dining room-kitchen-office-bedroom.

The wall on the left held my flat-screen and a watercolor painting I had found at a yard sale. On the right, a bookshelf housed an array of worn paperbacks. A bluebird-colored futon sat in the middle of the floor with a small desk behind it. Beyond the utilitarian living room/office, a kitchenette was squeezed into one corner and a nook into the other with just enough room in between for my emerald green Formica-topped table and four matching chairs. From the window, I had a view of the beautiful "downtown" area. For privacy, I had curtained off the nook, which held a makeshift closet and single bed. Not that I hold parties or have many visitors. Or any visitors. But you never know.

A quick glance at my phone and its blinking red light, let me know there was a message waiting for me. I had a funny feeling that I knew who it was, but I checked it anyway.

"Erica." The soothing voice of Susan Findlay, my therapist. "You've missed two group sessions in a row without giving notice. Please call me when you get a chance."

At least it wasn't my mother. *Thank God.* She had called once before in an outlandish attempt to fix me up with some "bright young man" who worked for a bank. The fact that my parents and I had spoken maybe twice since my return from overseas fazed my mother not at all. I made it crystal clear that I had no interest in her bright young man.

Neither of my parents understood why I joined the Marines. Frankly, it was to escape the oppressive relationship my parents had with me and with each other. My father was one of those men who always wanted a son, and my achievements were never good enough for him. He also tended to boss my Mom around. Her responses were mostly passive-aggressive, but she never really stood up to him either on my behalf or her own.

Returning Susan's call could wait, but not too long, because I needed to attend at least 25 sessions to officially establish my sobriety to the state's satisfaction. First, I wanted to follow up on my big new case while my motivation was high. I erased the message.

I was about to boot up my computer when a black squirrel climbed onto the kitchenette's window sill. He was such a frequent visitor, I had installed a sliding window screen so I could feed the little guy.

"Hey, Rocky," I said to the squirrel. "Want a peanut?"

Rocky gazed at me through the window as I fetched the jar of shelled nuts. He waited patiently while I opened the window and handed him one. As he stuffed it in his mouth, I placed a small pile of nuts on the sill and closed the window. Rocky filled his mouth with nuts until his cheeks were huge and lumpy.

After feeding my "pet" squirrel, I pondered my next move while waiting for my laptop to fire up. I logged into one of my paid databases and searched for Melissa's last known address. A Baltimore City address came up, so I made a note of it. Maybe worth a visit.

I tried calling Melissa myself, but there was no answer and no voice mail. Okay.

Since that first attempt failed, I did a reverse search on Melissa's last known address and came up with another number. OK, now we're talking.

Using my own landline (and hitting the code to conceal my number on the other end), I punched in the number and got a young-sounding woman on the second ring.

"Yes, hi," I said. "Could I speak with a Ms. Melissa Blaine, please?" I added the "Ms.", hoping to sound like the call was formal.

"I'm sorry," the young woman said. "She doesn't live here anymore."

"That's a shame," I said. "I work for the law firm Dewey and Associates. Ms. Blaine has inherited some money. Did she leave a forwarding address?"

"No, I'm sorry. The note she left with her last rent payment only said she was moving. She didn't even say goodbye." The young woman sounded more perplexed than upset.

"When was this?"

"Exactly two weeks ago," she said. "The rent was due that day."

Before she and Blaine had last spoken.

"And I take it you haven't heard from her?" I pressed on with ridiculous optimism.

"Not a word."

On that note, we exchanged pleasant farewells and I hung up. Back to the drawing board.

I considered calling Melissa's mother, but decided to hold off. Quizzing people by phone isn't my first choice, and if Melissa had sought refuge from her father in California, what was the likelihood that her mother would talk to me about it?

And what about art school? Plus flying to California to confirm anything exceeded my three-hour limit and then some.

The art school was quite accessible, and I could easily spare the time to poke around the campus..

Also, a talk with Katie Saunders seemed to be in order. She was away at college—not hugely helpful at narrowing my search.

I did another online search on the terms "Damascus High" and "Saunders". This time, I found a LinkedIn profile for Kathryn Saunders who had graduated from Damascus High School. Now taking graduate studies at Columbia University in New York City. The experience section showed that she worked as a teaching assistant in the English Department.

I called directory assistance for the Columbia University main number.

The woman who answered that number not only put me through to Katie's office, but gave me the direct number to call for future reference. The phone rang twice, and then a young woman answered. "English Department."

"Hello, is this Katie Saunders?"

"Yes. Who's this?"

I ditched the notion of using my class reunion ruse, because Katie would probably call me out on it.

"My name is Erica Jensen, and I'm looking for Melissa Blaine. I'm in one of her classes at MICA. She seems to have vanished. I understand you two were high school friends. Have you heard from her, by any chance?"

"No. It's been quite a while since Melissa and I last spoke. But you say she's disappeared?" Katie's tone struck me as worried.

"It would seem that way, miss." *Call her by her first name*, I thought. I silently berated myself for the excess formality. Two years of coaxing information from Afghan women, while making sure they are in fact women, should have taught me that. "Her father doesn't know where she is and hasn't heard from her, but he gave me your name. Any idea whether she might have decided to move without telling anyone?"

This was the notion that niggled at the back of my brain. Maybe Melissa didn't want to be found by her father. Would she tell anyone she knew, if she wanted to disappear completely?

"That doesn't sound like her," Katie assured me. "The last we spoke, Melissa was serious about attending the art school in Baltimore. I can't imagine her up and leaving there."

"When was the last time you saw or spoke to Melissa?"

A long pause ensued. "It was after my graduation," Katie said. "We had a girls' night out up here in New York, but that was years ago."

"Did she say or do anything back then that seemed unusual?"

"Unusual how?" Katie said. "I'm not sure what you mean. She was her usual self."

"Is she usually happy with her life?" I pressed on.

Katie issued a short, uncomfortable laugh. Like a coughed giggle. "Well, she's something of a temperamental artist. Melissa has her moods, but she didn't seem to be troubled the last time we got together. How did you say you knew her?"

"We're in the same class," I blurted. "I've been planning a project and we were going to work together."

"Ah." A non-committal utterance.

"Just out of curiosity, can you think of any reason she might want to hide from her father? He has no idea where she is."

"Oh, no." Katie's tone was dismissive. "Melissa depends on her father for financial support until after she turns twenty-five."

When her trust fund will free her from Blaine's hold.

"I understand her father didn't approve of her going to art school," I said.

"That's true, but I don't think he'd cut off her trust fund because of that."

I hate talking to people by phone. I had no way of gauging Katie's responses other than by her tone of voice. And even though New York was much closer to Maryland than California, a trek there would take all of the three hours I had pledged toward finding Melissa.

I racked my brain to think of what I should ask. This could be my last chance for information from this source. "One last question. Why would your sister be reluctant to talk to me about this? When I spoke to her about talking to you, she wouldn't give me the time of day."

Katie giggle-coughed again. "Probably being over-protective. She's my older sister, like a mother hen."

"I get that. Thanks for talking to me."

"No problem," she sang out. The line went dead.

CHAPTER FOUR

The church's basement reeked of overheated coffee and bleach. Despite my total lack of interest, I did call my therapist back and promise to make an appearance. I walked into the meeting room and surveyed the small group clustered around the coffee and donuts. It wasn't easy, but I stifled the urge to pump my fist and yell, "Let's get this party started!" Woo-hoo.

The group leader spotted me as she carefully arranged the chairs. She turned away from the chair project and walked toward me, waving.

"I'm so glad you're here, Erica," she said. "I've been worried about you."

I forced a smile. "Don't worry, be happy."

She leaned toward me and touched my arm. "Is this really so hard? I think you've come a long way since your discharge. I would hate to see you backslide into using again."

Susan was in her early thirties, maybe a few years older. She had shoulder-length, wavy blonde hair, bright blue eyes, and a creamy complexion. Today, she wore a green tunic and black leggings with short black boots. She looked like she had never suffered a sleepless night.

"Think I'll go get some bad coffee," I said. Anything to keep me awake.

Susan laughed. "Okay. We'll get started soon." She flitted off to fiddle more with the seating.

I crossed the room to the refreshments table. My support group of seven had grown by three more members in my absence. People were scattered about, chatting among themselves. Two of them—one Army grunt and a Marine—had also served in either Afghanistan or Iraq. As I poured a cup of the dark and no-doubt bitter brew, I felt a presence at my side.

"Hi. My name is Nick. This is only my second meeting. You just join?"

I looked up to see a man of about thirty, with unruly brown hair and dark eyes.

"My name is Erica, and this isn't my first time. It may be my last, but I say that every time."

Nick grinned and shook his head. "Wow, don't hold back on my account."

"I tend not to sugarcoat my views."

"I'll do my best not to piss you off," he said. "May I say that you are very pretty?"

Oh-kay. "Sure." I gave him my happy face. "It's the high cheekbones, you know. Everyone used to tell me I should be a model."

"I take it you aren't?"

"Hardly. I don't think it's a good idea to build a career on your looks." I sipped my coffee. Not as burnt-tasting as I'd expected. "My cheekbones are the happy result of a few Cherokee genes." No one in my family talked about it, though. One of my grandmothers brought the topic up, only to have it dropped for good. I hoped mightily that my Anglo ancestors hadn't raped a native.

"Dare I ask how you feel about the Redskins?"

"The same way I feel about football. I couldn't care less."

He flashed another smile. "What do you do?"

I leaned toward him. "I'd tell you, but then I'd have to kill you." I winked at him and walked away.

Chairs scraped the floor as everyone took their seat. I picked my own, leaving an empty chair on either side. Almost immediately, Nick sat down next to me. "Hello, again," he said. "Fancy finding you here."

I suppressed a sigh. "I'm no good at small talk. Sorry."

"Neither am I. But I'm intrigued with what you've said so far." He extended a hand. "My name is Nick Baxter. And yours is?"

"Erica Jensen." I put my hand into his warm, firm grip and we shook amiably. He had a direct, if somewhat piercing, gaze.

Was he hitting on me or just terribly curious?

"I used to be a *Washington Post* reporter," he said "I'm working freelance now. Or trying to since I'm a victim of layoffs. I also work part-time as a night manager at Olive Garden."

"Are you a freelance editor or writer?" I asked.

"Both. I'm taking whatever work I can get."

Uh oh. That explained his curiosity. Guard your tongue, Erica. "Best of luck with that. Things are tough, huh?"

"Let's talk about you instead. Seriously, do you work for the government or what?"

"Okay, let's get started," Susan piped up, just in the nick of time. "Who would like to share first?"

Nick's gaze lingered on me. I mouthed, "No."

CHAPTER FIVE

I made it through that session without slipping into a coma or getting on my knees and banging my head on my chair. Sitting and listening to other people whine on about personal shit seems like a huge waste of time, but I force myself to do it. It's an art, listening. All good private eyes need the skill. I once mastered it as part of my mission with the Corps.

Ever since my concussion, I have found it much harder to concentrate on what people are saying. I need to cultivate that skill again if I ever hope to have a future in the information research business. For good or ill, group therapy forces me to pay attention and listen to others. Even though it feels like torment, I basically have no choice but to go to group therapy. So I attend with reluctance.

When it was Nick's turn to share, he intimated that he'd gone through a brief period of addiction to over-the-counter drugs. He said he was off the pills and into meditation, and his story seemed genuine.

As he spoke, I sensed a bit of anxiety. There was a disarming honesty in the way he revealed his insecurity about his future prospects. I didn't have to be an empath to understand that.

Nick asked me for my phone number after the session was over. I gave it to him with the hope that he wouldn't turn out to be one of those douchebags who use self-help groups to meet women. Time would tell.

The next day, I drove to MICA to see if anyone there could provide a clue as to Melissa Blaine's whereabouts. I circled through the maze of streets around the school, looking for a place to park. After about five minutes of driving around, a spot opened up just a block or so from the campus.

There were no coffee shops with the name Blaine had supplied as Melissa's employer, but I was betting she didn't work at Starbucks. There were, however, a few cafes near the school. I picked one at random that was squeezed between two much larger buildings across from the campus.

Naturally, my first try was a bust. But the second was a charm.

Java Joe's was a funky hole-in-the-wall, furnished with an overstuffed sofa and chairs, plus wooden tables and seats. Art decorated the walls, no doubt the work of promising MICA students, and a bookshelf jammed with used books sat in a corner.

Two people stood behind the counter—a young woman at a noisy espresso machine and a man behind the register. I approached the young man who was unoccupied at the moment and introduced myself. A white name tag pinned to his shirt identified him as "Steve." I launched into the spiel I'd prepared about how I was a friend of the family and that Melissa had vanished without a trace. Steve confirmed that Melissa worked there.

"Do you remember the last time you saw her here?" I asked.

Steve thought about it for a few seconds. "Maybe a couple of weeks ago. We usually work different shifts. Maybe Elle's seen her more recently."

He looked over at the drink-maker. "Hey, Elle," he called. "Have you seen Melissa Blaine lately?"

Elle shot us a puzzled look. She finished the drink she was working on, put it out on the counter, and called a name. "Who wants to know?" she asked, walking toward us as she wiped her hands on her red apron.

Steve jerked a thumb at me. "Her name's Erica. A friend of Melissa's family. Says she's missing."

Elle eyeballed me, up and down. "You a cop?"

"No, no. I'm not with the police. Melissa's old enough so the cops won't act unless there's some indication that she's in trouble."

Elle squinted at me, then nodded. "I thought Melissa quit. Last time she was here, it sounded like she wasn't planning to come back."

"Do you recognize either of these men?" I asked, showing them the photo of Slava Kandinsky and Stuart Blaine.

"Yeah," Elle said.

"Me, too," Steve piped up.

"That guy," Elle pointed to Kandinsky, "has been here several times. We call him Mr. Macchiato. But I haven't seen him lately."

"Do you remember when you last saw him? Was he with Melissa?" I asked.

Elle tilted her head. "Well, it's been a while. But I don't remember seeing him with Melissa."

"How about you?" I turned to Steve, who was shaking his head.

"I haven't seen him, but I've seen the other guy. Not in here, but I've seen him around."

"At the art school?"

"Yeah, that's it. I'm pretty sure I've seen him there."

"With Melissa?" I pressed on.

He shrugged. "Not that I recall."

"Can you remember where he was or what he was doing?"

Steve's brow creased with thought. "I just know the face is familiar."

"Do either of you know any of Melissa's close friends? Anyone she hangs with?"

Steve shrugged again, but Elle nodded. "She and Jen Gardiner hang out together. Jen also attends MICA. We all do here, pretty much. The school is, like, the cheap labor camp for the stores in this area." She smiled and gave me a wry look.

"Hmm. Great." I jotted the name. "You wouldn't know how to contact Jen, would you?"

"No. Sorry."

"No problem." I fished two cards from my shoulder bag and handed one to each of them. "Could you let me know if you hear from Melissa or Jen? Or think of anything else that might help me find Melissa?"

"Sure," Elle said.

"Absolutely," Steve added.

"Oh, and a medium latte. To go, please."

The espresso machine roared into action as I considered the new information. Stuart Blaine could have come here to see his daughter. As for Kandinsky . . . there could be any number of reasons. My best bet was to start by exploring that connection.

Who knows, I thought. *Maybe I could kill two birds with one stone here.*

CHAPTER SIX

Before I looked for Kandinsky, I figured I'd visit MICA while I was in the neighborhood. So before I left Java Joe's, I asked if there was an instructor at the school who might be helpful.

"Now that you mention it," Steve said, "there is one that everyone likes. Marie Solomon. She mentors a lot of students. Melissa might be one. You could see if she knows anything."

"Thanks, I will." I lifted my latte cup in farewell.

The art school is spread over several blocks of the Bolton Hill area, and the logical place to start seemed like the administration building, a solid, white block of classical architecture. The high-ceilinged, columned foyer surrounded a marble stairway built to impress. One staircase led down from each side of the second floor, they met in the middle and then descended as a single staircase that widened right before it reached the first floor. If I squinted, the steps seemed to create illusory ripples, as if the stairway had managed to liquefy.

Students milled about, artwork or portfolios tucked under their arms. Chatter bounced off the granite walls, creating a constant thrum.

Finding the main office was easy enough. A young woman with Rit-dyed red hair was happy to point me toward it. Even the clerk behind the counter seemed cheerful. She directed me to Marie Solomon's office with a smile and a twinkle in her eyes. Maybe I should get a job at MICA. Then I could be perky all the time, too.

I climbed the stairs, turned left at the top, and walked to the second door on the right. The door was open, and I heard quiet conversation, so I decided to peek inside. A tall, thin woman in her thirties stood with a younger woman—probably a student. I hung back and waited. Eventually, the instructor and student came to the door, and when the younger one left, the woman I assumed was Marie Solomon beamed at me. "How can I help you?"

After exchanging introductions, I gave her the spiel and asked if she'd seen Melissa recently.

Marie Solomon's smile faded. "The last time I saw her was two weeks ago, as of last Friday."

"You seem sure of the date."

The instructor nodded. "I'm sure of it, but I'll double-check my calendar, if you like."

As she spoke, Solomon walked to her desk calendar and flipped the pages back. *Ooh, paper instead of pixels.* Call me old-fashioned, but I have a genuine love for all things paper, not to mention a huge distrust of technology.

"There," she said, pointing to the page. "I saw her at 1:30, exactly two weeks ago Friday."

"Can you tell me what you discussed, without violating any privacy rules?"

The woman frowned. "No, I really can't. But you say she's disappeared?" Pausing for a moment, she added, "Are you with the police?"

"I'm not a cop," I assured her. "Just a concerned friend of the family."

"I'm not sure how much I'm at liberty to say."

"Well, if it helps any, I'm not too crazy about Melissa's dad," I said. "But if nothing else, I'd like to make sure she's okay."

Marie Solomon looked me over as if appraising me. "In that case, I can tell you this much. Melissa seemed upset when we met. She mentioned possibly taking a break from school. I was concerned, of course, and tried to talk her out of it, but if she wanted to quit that was her choice.

"Since then, I haven't seen her in class or anywhere around the school." She stared over my shoulder, her gaze puzzled. "I suspect she might have dropped out." Solomon raised her hand in physical punctuation. "I haven't received official word on that, though," she cautioned.

I wondered whether I dared to press my inquiries any further, but I forged ahead. "I understand Melissa is good friends with another student, Jen Gardiner. Have you ever talked to her about Melissa?"

Solomon shook her head, gaze drifting down. "Sorry. I'm already cutting things close to the line. Besides, I really don't have a clue where Melissa is."

Giving it one last try, I asked, "Did Melissa mention her father or a man named Slava Kandinsky?"

"No. Who's Slava Kandinsky?"

I'm not a mind reader, but Solomon's reaction suggested she was telling the truth.

"No one you need to worry about," I said, hoping that I was right.

CHAPTER SEVEN

I had promised Blaine three hours and no more to find Melissa. However, hearing that Kandinsky, supposedly the main focus of my investigation, had been hanging around the art school raised a red flag or at least presented the possibility that Melissa and Kandinsky knew one another better than my client thought. It could have been a coincidence, but I'm not a big believer in that. Even so, I couldn't jump to any conclusion based on what little I knew at that point.

Nonetheless, I had a name—Jen Gardiner. To save on minutes of data usage, I sought out the nearest free wi-fi connection and did a simple directory search on Gardiner's name. Couldn't even come up with a J. Gardiner, but I did find the name on Facebook. Location: Baltimore City. The avatar: a flower. That's helpful. I would need to check my subscription databases for more.

At that point, I had to make a choice. I could wander around the campus asking random bystanders about Melissa and Jen Gardiner, or I could move on to what I thought should be my priority—investigating Kandinsky. I went back to my car and checked my file for Kandinsky's home address. He lived in

Ellicott City. Not exactly around the corner from Java Joe's. Talk about a red flag.

Before I drove to Kandinsky's house, I updated my research diagram with a new shape representing Jen Gardiner and added a dotted line between the symbols for Melissa and Kandinsky. If Melissa's disappearance was related to the alleged embezzlement, so much for the three-hour limit.

About half an hour later, I pulled up in front of a brick rambler set behind a lawn as lush and manicured as a putting green. I got out of the car and walked up the driveway toward a set of flat stones leading to the front door. The neighborhood was eerily quiet and the air held the musty odor of marigolds. The traffic noise from nearby Route 40 was oddly subdued. I rang the bell and waited.

After a few minutes, I rang the bell again and knocked hard on the door. My knock sent the door swinging open, so I poked my head inside. The air conditioning must have been turned up to maximum freeze, because the house was as cold as a meat locker.

I hesitated for a minute, and then went in. There were no cars in the driveway. Kandinsky could have made tracks with the money and Melissa. But why would he leave the air conditioning on and at full blast to boot?

It didn't take long to find the answer. As I moved from the foyer into the living room, I passed the kitchen and caught a glimpse of a body sprawled on the floor. Being careful not to touch anything, I approached the prone form of the man to confirm that it was, in fact, Slava Kandinsky. He'd been shot at least twice. The bullets had punched holes through the back of his shirt and the base of his skull. Blood, sticky and dark, had leaked from the head wound and congealed in a grim aureola.

I heard the sound of a passing car (sounded larger than a car—a delivery truck maybe?) and absent-mindedly catalogued it, along with the gory vision before me. A sudden loud bang made me jerk to attention. My heart raced. For a moment, I was back in the desert again. I stood stock still and took several deep breaths, trying to slow down my pounding heart. All was quiet now. *Had the passing vehicle hit a pothole? Or had someone fired off an M-80?* I peeked out the kitchen window, which had a view of the street. No movement. No fireworks. All clear.

I returned to the body, squatted, and studied it. Kandinsky's head faced left, as if he was turning to look at me. I spotted a third entry wound. The bullet had plunged clean through his temple, the entry wound was a small hole with no visible powder burns. His skin was waxy and bluish. I didn't dare touch his shirt, but I was willing to bet that the torso shot went through his lung or even his heart. I'm no medical examiner, but I've seen enough dead people to recognize a professional killing.

I stood up and edged around Kandinsky to check the wall for bullet holes. None that I could see. The small, white kitchen appeared otherwise undisturbed. I snatched a paper towel off the rack and, using it to prevent leaving fingerprints, checked drawers and cabinets. The kitchen wasn't likely where Kandinsky had kept receipts, but you never know what you'll find or where.

The cupboards were well-stocked, as was the fridge. I noticed butter pecan ice cream in the freezer and resisted the temptation to take it home.

After further checking the kitchen, I searched each of the other rooms. The furnishings were standard Ikea, geared toward comfort rather than style. My cursory search revealed nothing, but then the killer might have taken the money or any account records. Or not.

Apart from hoping that I could find the money, I was focused on finding clues. I didn't know exactly what I was looking for, but anything linking Kandinsky to Melissa would definitely be a plus.

I had a pair of leather driving gloves in my car. I mentally debated retrieving and wearing them before conducting a more thorough search of the house versus getting the hell out of there.

Duty calls, I reminded myself, and went to fetch the gloves. I could only hope that no curious neighbors shielded by window curtains were watching me.

I donned the gloves, returned to the house, and searched each room again. This time, I was more thorough, looking under the seat cushions of the living room furniture, as well as between the mattress and box springs on the bed. I shivered because the house was so cold, but I didn't dare open a window or touch the Thermostat. I knew the stink of a dead man's body would increase along with the rise in temperature.

The bathroom revealed nothing useful. Kandinsky had recently used a decongestant. An open package of nasal spray lay across the washstand. The pollen from ragweed will kill you this time of year . . . unless somebody with a gun gets you first..

I booted up the computer in what looked to be Kandinsky's home office. However, in order to access anything, I needed the password. Damn. It could take forever to guess, and I didn't want to accidentally lock myself out.

I upended waste paper baskets and pawed through the contents. Found an envelope addressed to Kandinsky, but no letter or return address. The handwriting was plain, block letter print. Very tidy.

I dug into the bedroom closet. A stack of folded papers bound with thick rubber bands hid behind a box on a shelf. Setting them on the bed, I eased one page out. It was a handwritten letter, the paper off-white and the writing neat and clear, but it appeared to have been written in Russian or some Cyrillic script.

I looked again and found one I could read. Based on the salutation and signature, it was a letter from Kandinsky's son. It was dated a month ago and consisted of three sentences.

Dear Dad,

I'm sorry, but I can't do what you've asked. I have to live my life the way I see fit. I hope you understand.

Love,
David

So, Kandinsky had a son, and apparently the father disagreed with the son's life choices. An old story, if there ever was one— my story in fact. But what had Kandinsky asked of David? Did what Kandinsky ask lead to his own murder?

It occurred to me that Kandinsky's son and Blaine's daughter both had parent issues. Mere coincidence? Had Blaine even mentioned Kandinsky's son?

Abandoning the search for the moment, I left the house. The street was as quiet and empty as when I'd gone in, but the clock was ticking. Commuters would soon be returning home from work. Even housekeepers or nannies in the neighborhood might become suspicious.

I returned to my car and checked the notes I took at Blaine's house to see if he had mentioned Kandinsky's son. Couldn't recall him doing so and saw no mention of David there, but I noticed something else. I forgot that Blaine said it had been four days since he'd heard from Melissa. Based on what Melissa's art instructor and her co-workers at Java Joe's had said, she had been absent from school roughly two weeks. Why this time discrepancy?

CHAPTER EIGHT

I extracted my cell phone from my shoulder bag and called Blaine, leaving a message to get in touch with me as soon as possible. Then, I went back inside the Kandinsky house.

The time disparity between Melissa's last phone call with her father and the day she was last seen at school worried me. Perhaps Melissa's pride kept her from revealing that she had stopped going to class. After all, her father hadn't approved of her career plans.

I considered other possibilities. Had someone taken Melissa and forced her to call her father? Toward what end? I needed to get more details from Blaine about their last conversation. Given the circumstances, I had no reason to think he would hold anything back.

Just in case, I used my cell phone to take photos of the letters and put them back their proper place with the other papers. When I tucked the bundle back into the closet, I noticed a small blue binder with the words "Cherished Memories" embossed in gold on the cover. I picked it up and flipped through the plastic-encased photos inside. In a few of them, I saw Kandinsky posed with a woman. I also found photos with

Kandinsky, the woman and a boy. Probably the son, David. One picture resembled a high school yearbook headshot of the boy, now a teenager. Based on the contents, it seemed that Kandinsky had fathered only one child.

I slid the most recent photo of David from its holder, set it on the dresser, and snapped a shot of it with my cell. I did the same for one photo of the woman. The closet in which I had found the photo album contained only men's clothes. If Kandinsky and his wife or live-in girlfriend had been estranged, how hard did either of them take it? Did the presence of a woman in his life (or the lack thereof) pertain to his death?

After tucking the photo album away, I continued to search the closet and scanned the room. A brightly colored Russian nesting doll, of all things, sat on a bedside table. On a hunch, I took it apart. Inside the smallest doll, I found a key. I'd be skating on mighty thin ice if I took it. What would I do with it anyway?

For lack of other options, I tore a page from the notebook in my shoulder bag. Pressing the paper onto the key, I took a pencil and ran the point sideways, back and forth, atop it. I managed to make a very rough outline of the key's shape, ridges and indentations. Turning it over, I repeated the process. Far from perfect, but it would have to do.

I also took a photo of the key and noted the alphanumeric code engraved on it. With this information, maybe a locksmith could provide a lead on what the key opened.

I slipped out the door and hurried to my car, leaving Kandinsky's body for someone else to find.

On Route 40, one of Ellicott City's main roads, I found a Home Depot. Whether I'd find a real locksmith there was another question. I decided to take my chances, so I pulled into the shopping center's parking lot.

I had a hunch the key opened a safe deposit box. If so, then getting access could be a problem. Unless I could track down Kandinsky's son or the woman who appeared to be his wife. In any case, Kandinsky's death left someone as his heir. Maybe more than one someone.

I found an elderly man who made keys in the hardware section. Unfortunately, he had no more clue than I did about what the key would unlock, but he was able to tell me where to find the nearest locksmith—right in the heart of old town.

I left the store and headed down Route 40 to Rogers Road, which led to the county courthouses. Taking a right, then another, I ended up on Ellicott City's Main Street. This part of town had suffered a series of devastating floods over the years, but had somehow managed to endure. Whether the history of old town Ellicott City merited the residents' continued allegiance to doing business there—come flood, come whatever—had escalated into an ongoing controversy. The place was an environmental disaster area and a journalist's dream.

The narrow road was lined with historic buildings, crammed together. It plunged downhill in a set of curves, past a rocky outcropping, toward the old mill and the railroad bridge. The locksmith's shop was wedged between a tobacconist store and a place that sold used hippie clothes.

Main Street's crowded curbs left me no place to park my car. I ended up leaving it in a small lot alongside the bridge and walking down the hill toward the shop. As I approached, the stench of patchouli from the hippie store nearly knocked me on my ass.

My entrance into the locksmith's shop set the small chime-like bell hung over the door to ringing. A man in his early 20s or younger stood behind the counter, organizing stock. Was he the locksmith? He was just a kid, but then so was everyone I'd served with in Afghanistan.

The young man came to attention and said, "May I help you?"

"Hi," I said. "I'm trying to figure out what this key unlocks. Would you be able to tell me?" I showed him the photo, the outline of the key, and the information I'd noted on the key itself.

"The key to a safe," he said, with barely a look at the photo.

"How can you tell?"

"The manufacturer's number you wrote down. Hudson makes keys for standalone safes."

I squinted at him. "I'm not doubting you, but I need to be sure. Are you positive?"

"Let me take another look," he said. He glanced at it again and nodded vigorously. "The shape is right, too. Take my word for it. I can look up the specific model, if you like."

"You said it was a standalone. So it's movable?"

"Could be. Depends on who's moving it."

How about a dead Russian's wife or ex-wife? Thoughts best left unspoken. "Is it possible to make a copy of the key, using this etching?" I asked instead.

"I'm sorry. There are high-tech ways, but we don't have those here. I'd need either the key or an impression of it."

My heart sank a bit. Time to make another command decision.

CHAPTER NINE

As I trudged uphill toward my car, I wondered where the safe might be located. I could've sworn I had checked every inch of Kandinsky's house. Maybe his killer made off with the safe. If so, surely they'd find a way to force it open.

However, if the killer didn't have the safe, it had to be somewhere accessible to Kandinsky. I'd checked the attic and basement. Maybe it was buried in the yard or under a floorboard. Was it worth returning there, not only to take another look, but to make a waxed impression of the key?

I unlocked the car, got inside, and sat there, staring through the windshield. My head slowly filled with a jumble of thoughts, which were mostly suppositions. For all I knew, Kandinsky had siphoned off the money to an account in the Bahamas. I was not at all sure the key was worth all this mental effort, so I turned my mind to other matters.

Did Kandinsky steal the money, as Blaine suspected? And if so, how? And did he have an accomplice? On top of that, why was he hanging out at the coffee shop where Melissa worked?

I pulled my flowchart from the file and gazed at the diagram. It had nothing new to offer.

Right now, my best leads were the letters and photos I'd found in Kandinsky's closet. Since I couldn't read a word of Russian, I needed a translator. My friend Two-Bit Terry claimed to know almost every one of the world's current languages.

Two-Bit Terry was the name the then 20-year-old Terry Morris acquired while performing on the Ocean City boardwalk. I had known him since high school where we shared the status of "invisible nerds." I spent my lunch break with my face buried in a graphic novel whereas Terry had learned to read at age 3 and seemed to know a little bit about everything.

In Ocean City, Terry was one of those guys who guesses your weight and age, within a certain range of possibilities (plus or minus whatever number Terry had devised). But first you had to pay him a quarter. If you stumped him, he'd give out a cheap prize. If he was right, no prize. Terry had good intuition, and all those two-bit wins added up.

Unfortunately, he had no license to perform on the Boardwalk. This led to a few misunderstandings with the local police. It was Ocean City's finest who had endowed Terry with a nickname worthy of a bit part in *Guys and Dolls*. Rather than reject it, Terry relished the idea of being such an official pain in the ass that he had (in his own words) "acquired the moniker." So Terry began using it on a regular basis, even after leaving Ocean City for more promising opportunities. He thought his old nickname lent him a certain gravitas. Two-Bit Terry may have been a genius, but his idea of gravitas was kinda messed up.

None of that mattered, at the moment. I needed a translator, and Terry could probably do the job.

I tried to raise him on the phone. His voice mail was full. Weird.

I fired up the car and headed toward Laurel. Last I heard, Terry worked from home as an On-Call Geek fixing computers and doing other cyber stuff. After a quick spin down Route 29, plus a fifteen-minute drive after exiting the main highway, I pulled into a space near Two-Bit's apartment. His car sat nearby.

It was late afternoon, and I hoped Terry would answer the door. I clanged up the metal steps to reach his third floor flat. Knocking gently on the door, I waited.

When there was no response, I knocked louder. Still nothing. His car was in the lot, which worried me.

I fished a bump key from my shoulder bag. In the old days, only locksmiths had these. But now, anyone can buy them online. Terry's not exactly a health nut. His notion of a balanced meal is to have fries with his burger. Hopefully, if Terry was in there, passed out or worse, I was in time to help.

After inserting the key, I wiggled and smacked it lightly with my small notebook until the lock turned. I opened the door, stepped inside, and froze.

Terry sat on the sofa—the biggest piece of furniture in his sparsely-decorated living room—pointing a gun at me. He was tall and skinny, with disheveled light brown hair. In his baggy jeans and loose-fitting T-shirt, he looked like a criminal scarecrow.

A feeling of deva vu and an adrenaline rush washed through me. If Terry hadn't been a familiar face, I might have taken serious defensive measures. Thank God I didn't have a weapon.

He lowered the gun. "C'mon in," he said. "Sorry about that." He set the weapon down on the coffee table.

"Expecting guests, Terry?" I asked, after finding my voice.

There's something about walking into a friend's home and finding the occupant pointing a gun at you. It tends to throw you off.

"Good thing I'm not carrying, huh?" I added, pouring on the sarcasm.

Terry approached me, a flush of shame spreading across his face. He extended a tentative hand. When I didn't slap it away, he placed it on my arm.

"I'm really sorry, Erica," he said. "I just need to be prepared."

"Prepared for what?" I glanced at the gun, grimacing. "You setting someone up for an ambush?" Didn't seem like Terry's style.

He waved a hand. "Just a couple of knuckleheads who think I hacked into their system. They've been getting nasty. And, yeah, I'm thinking they might be making an unannounced visit at some point."

"And you're going to stay here and provide a reception?" I asked. "Why not hide out in a motel for a while? Or get a better lock for your door?" *Uh, who's the real knucklehead here?*

"I can defend myself, but I can't hide in motels forever. I figured, okay, fine, if you want to play it that way, let's get it done with." Terry strolled to the door, locked the doorknob lock and threw the deadbolt securely into place. Apparently, Terry had conveniently left that unlocked for his unwanted guests. "But, forget about that. Let's talk."

"Yeah, let's. I tried to call. How long have you ignored your voice mail? I couldn't even leave a message."

Terry picked up his phone. "A while, yeah. Got tired of taking calls from those dipshits I mentioned." He grinned. "Sorry."

"This won't take long," I assured him, my eyes darting from the door to him and back. "I just wanted to ask you to translate this letter. It looks like Russian, but I'm no expert."

I thumbed to the photo of the letter on my cell phone. Terry squinted at the screen. "Let's take a closer look," he said. He strolled down a short hall, with me in tow and took the first right into his home office. A computer was parked by the window, its psychedelic screensaver in constant motion.

Terry jiggled the mouse, then scrabbled through a small pile of cables, pulling out a thin one to hook my phone up to his computer And with a few key taps and mouse clicks, he transferred the photo to his computer and enlarged it.

After one quick look, he nodded. "Yeah, I'd say you're sorta right. It's actually a bastardized version of Georgian. As in the former Soviet Georgia." Terry looked at it more closely and frowned. "Where did you get this?" he asked.

I cleared my throat. "I found it."

Terry leaned back in his chair and stared at me. "Not in your mailbox, I hope."

"Of course not. It's not addressed to me, is it?"

Terry shrugged. "No, but it's addressed to . . . well, not a nice word. It would translate roughly to 'Jerkoff.' Or the Georgian version of it."

"So, uh, what does the letter say?"

Terry sighed and stared back at the screen. In a halting manner, as if struggling a bit with the odd use of language, he read: "Dear Jerkoff, It's been nearly a week since we last talked. You are way overdue at this point. You will either pay us in full by the end of the month or you will get an unwelcome visitor. You know how this works. We're very disappointed in you. One with such a stellar record as you should know better. Don't bother to answer without payment included."

Terry continued, his eyes glued to the screen. "It pains me to write this letter, since we've always been friendly, but what you've done is unacceptable." He paused, squinting at the page. "Business is business. End of discussion."

Terry turned from the computer toward me. "The letter ends there."

CHAPTER TEN

"Interesting," I said. "What do you make of this?"

"Well, obviously, someone threatened the intended recipient . . . "

"I got that much," I said. "Does it sound like it was written by someone in the Russian mob?"

Terry peered at the screen. "Well . . . not necessarily."

"Why do you say that?"

Terry scratched his head and leaned back in his chair. "The writing itself suggests otherwise. This isn't written in Russian. It's written in Georgian, which is similar, but not the same. A whole 'nuther country now. I don't know if they have ties to the Russian mob or not."

"Perhaps the letter was written by someone connected to the Mob who isn't Russian," I said.

"Good point," Terry said. "Or maybe 'Jerkoff' knows Georgian.

"The letter doesn't prove anything, really." He lifted his long, gangly arm and let it drop.

"It's the only lead I have right now."

"Lead on what?" he asked.

"Better that you don't know," I replied. "Based on the reception you gave me when I arrived, it looks like you've got enough trouble already."

I thought back to my meeting with Blaine. I didn't recall him mentioning that Kandinsky had a drug habit or gambling debts. Not only that, but I'd run a background check on both Blaine and his partner before the meeting on Monday—a mere two days ago, although it felt like a week. I always like to know who I'm doing business with. True to their claim, the partners appeared to run a clean shop. Neither had been arrested, not counting Blaine's previous incarceration.

"Look, I'd like to explore this Russian-Georgian or whatever angle further," I said. "What do you know about the Russian mob?"

"Enough to steer clear of them. That's about all."

I must have looked terribly frustrated, because he added, "I do know someone who might know more."

φφφ

I left Terry's apartment armed with a printed copy of the letter and a new contact: George Kirov, Professor of Criminology at the University of Maryland. Terry mentioned that Kirov knew first-hand about mobs (Russian and otherwise) from his time working for the FBI. I kept that in the back of my mind as I mulled over the questions I wanted to ask him.

Before I started my car, I checked the notes from my meeting with Blaine again. Just as I remembered, Blaine had simply asked me to find Kandinsky and the missing money. He never mentioned reasons why Kandinsky might have stolen it. Why would he? And how could he know?

I left the parking lot and headed home. By now, the sun was low in the sky. My interview with Professor Kirov would have to wait until tomorrow.

I'd driven no more than half a mile when my cell phone rang. One hand on the wheel, I used the other to hit the speakerphone button.

"Erica, I'm returning your call." It was Stuart Blaine, sounding fatigued.

"Would you mind if I stopped by for a moment?" I asked. "I have a few more questions."

"Can't you ask me now?"

"I'd prefer that we meet. I promise it won't take more than a few minutes."

He let out a loud sigh. "Okay, fine ."

"Be there in about thirty." I started to say goodbye, but Blaine had already hung up.

Much as I wanted to call it a day, I could manage to swing by Blaine's on the way home. The trip gave me time to consider my questions, how to frame them and how much to ask. I could already tell that the kind of conversation we would be having would benefit from face-to-face contact. I was as interested in his reaction as I was in what he would say.

By the time I turned into Blaine's driveway, the sun had disappeared behind the trees. The mini-manse appeared as dark and foreboding as a Gothic manor.

After I rang the doorbell, it only took seconds for Blaine to answer. He was dressed in a ratty T-shirt and worn jeans. Always the dapper one.

"Hi. Thanks for agreeing to see me," I said.

"Ask your questions." *You're welcome. Guess I'm not getting the Grand Tour this time.*

I breathed in and exhaled slowly to maintain my composure. "How well did you know Slava Kandinsky?"

Blaine crossed his arms and leaned against the door frame. "Well enough to trust him as a business partner."

"Would you say you were friends?"

"Friendly, yes. Close friends? Well . . ." His mouth set in a firm line. "We don't talk much about our personal lives, if that's what you mean."

"Was he married? Did he have a son or other children?"

"I . . . I really . . . I don't know." Blaine had the good grace to look ashamed. Then, his eyes widened and he asked, "Why do you keep talking about him as if he's . . . " His voice trailed off.

"As if he's dead?" I looked directly at Blaine, scrutinizing him. "Because he is. I found him shot to death at his home."

"Dear God." He whispered the words. His look transformed to one of fear. "Did you call the police?"

"I didn't think it advisable, given your strong preference against involving the police."

He nodded. "Thank you." Blaine seemed less upset than relieved.

"Now will you tell me exactly how you decided to become partners?"

Blaine stood up straight and shifted away from the door frame. "I met him at a local business mixer. We seemed to hit it off well enough, so after checking out his credentials, I asked him to meet me privately. That's when I first proposed our partnership."

"And, no doubt, he knew of your legal . . . escapades?" I pressed further.

Blaine gave me a look that suggested I'd lost a few marbles. "Everyone did. Does. Your point?"

I kept my eyes on him, gauging his every move and vocal intonation. "To the best of your knowledge, was Slava Kandinsky connected in any way with organized crime?"

"I found nothing in his background to suggest that."

"Did you ever cross paths with organized criminals, during," I paused to mentally revise my thought. "Before you were incarcerated?"

"No." His tone was flat, his expression changing from an inquisitive squint to a scowl. "I've done my time, and I don't do business with crooks."

My questions seemed to be leading nowhere. If he was lying, I doubted that he would simply break down and confess if I kept going down this road.

"Let me ask you something," he said, stabbing a finger at me. "Have you made any progress in finding my daughter?"

I took a moment to breathe again, for fear I might bark at him. "Mr. Blaine, you hired me all of two days ago." God knows, it felt like forever. "I told you then, I'd devote three hours of my time toward that task. I am still in the middle of completing my entire assignment for you. And, per our contract, I'll send you a report of my findings by week's end."

"OK, OK," he said, waving a hand. All debonnaire now. "I'm just concerned about her. Like any parent would be."

"Okay, then." I tried my best to sound conciliatory, but I still didn't quite trust the man. His responses seemed a bit too blasé.

"So." Blaine spat the word out. "Are we done here?"

"Yes, thank you. We can talk later."

I turned and left before he could slam the door in my face.

CHAPTER ELEVEN

The next day, I looked up Professor George Kirov in the university's online directory. I called his office and made an appointment to meet him later that morning.

In the interim, I searched online for David Kandinsky. The name did not pop up in the usual phone directories. Perhaps David relied on his cell phone. Not unusual these days.

So, I went into a credit database to see what I could find. Believe it or not, there was a long list of David Kandinsky's. At least twenty, scattered here and there around the country. Imagine how many more there might be outside the United States.

There had to be a way to narrow down the possible sons of Slava Kandinsky. I realized once the cops found out about Kandinsky's death, they'd find a way to contact his next of kin. Quite likely, they would end up contacting David. Or Slava's wife or ex-wife. I decided to let the cops do the work and somehow get the intel from them later.

Before I left for Kirov's office, I checked myself in my full-length mirror. My black slacks, matching jacket, and pin-striped button down shirt looked professional. My dark, shoulder-length hair was behaving for once and framed my face nicely. I checked my teeth. Nothing gross stuck in there, so I grabbed the file and walked out to my car.

The drive to the University of Maryland College Park campus was unusually free of traffic. I made it there in record time, which was lucky given the amount of time it took to find a parking spot.

Kirov's office was in LeFrak Hall, a colonial-style, red-brick building typical of others on campus. I parked my car a few hundred miles from the building and did a long march across the wide green slope criss-crossed by paths that fronts the campus. Once I reached the building, I took the stairs to the second floor, per Kirov's instructions, and managed to find his office. I knocked on the door and heard a deep voice call, "Come in."

Kirov stood behind his desk. He was tall, with ink-black hair and dazzling blue eyes. I judged him to be in his early 50s. The professor had a cozy office decorated with dark wood furniture and a multi-colored Persian rug. Bookshelves lined the walls, and I half expected to see a fire in an open fireplace.

"Come on in. Have a seat," he said, his voice booming. "I assume you're Erica Jensen?" We exchanged the usual niceties, and then I chose a guest chair that faced his desk and retrieved a writing pad from the file and a pen from my shoulder bag.

Kirov eased into his high-back chair and spread his arms wide. "How can I help you today? You said something on the phone about Russian mobsters, right?"

I explained once again about the letter I'd found and my questions about the Russian mob and the use of the Georgian language.

"Ah, yes," he said, steepling his fingers. "May I see the letter?"

I fished it from the file and handed it to him.

He frowned as he read it. "Interesting. This is written in a weird combination of Russian and Georgian."

"So I've been told," I said, eager to get to the heart of the matter. "Could you read it aloud?"

"I can give you the gist."

Kirov gave a reading that was virtually identical to Terry's.

"Thanks," I said. "Does the Russian mob have any connection to Georgia?"

"The Russian mafia makes connections wherever and however it suits their purpose," he said, putting the letter down. "If they found a way to make a profit through a former Soviet nation, they'd do it.

He paused, frowning at the letter, as if in disapproval. "Have you ever heard of a place called Svaneti?"

"No. Never."

"I ask because the letter is so oddly written. As I said, neither Russian nor Georgian. As if the author wasn't sure how to express himself or herself to the recipient." He raised a finger, as if to begin a lesson. "Svaneti is an unusual place for several reasons. For one thing, it's located way up in the Caucasus Mountains. Very few people live there, let alone go there. Plus, Svan is a dialect of Georgian. It's an oral language only and nearly dead."

"You know a lot about the Russian culture," I observed. "Did you learn all this as a criminologist?"

"I know this as one who focused on Russian studies before attending law school," he answered. "I've had a life-long fascination for my genealogical roots and my forebears' culture."

I hummed assent and nodded. "So, what else makes this Swameti interesting?"

Kirov gave me a mock glare. "It's Svaneti," he said, mildly. "It's a medieval village, walled in like a fortress. The Svans were known as fierce warriors for centuries, dating back to the sixth century AD. In the early eleventh century, Svaneti became a duchy within Georgia. When the Mongols invaded Georgia, Svaneti became a safe house for Georgian artifacts. Because the village is so high up in the mountains and the paths there so difficult to traverse, the Georgians in the lowlands moved precious icons, jewels, and manuscripts to Svaneti to keep them out of enemy hands."

I perked up. "Any possibility the Russian mafia might deal in smuggling such items into this country?"

He smiled like a pleased tutor. "More than a possibility. I wouldn't doubt it for a moment."

CHAPTER TWELVE

Professor Kirov turned out to be a gold mine of information. He also seemed eager and happy to share. I settled in for a lecture.

"You see," Kirov continued. "Smuggling artifacts—or cultural property, as it's generally called—is among the top ten most profitable crimes. And the United States is one of the top markets for illicit cultural property of all kinds. You're probably aware that the Washington area has quite a few museums."

"I've heard there's a little place called the Smithsonian," I chimed in, unable to resist.

"Yes, but not just the Smithsonian. There are private museums, as well as cultural and historical societies throughout the Baltimore-D.C. area."

Brief thoughts of the cultural artifacts from the Middle East floated through my head. I vaguely recalled a line from *Full Metal Jacket*, "I came to Vietnam to meet people of an ancient culture and kill them."

"Don't museums need proof of ownership before they'll buy something?" I asked.

"Provenance? Yes, but such papers can be forged."

"And they accept them at face value?"

Kirov shrugged. "Depends on the price. The institution. Not all museum curators are created equal. Not only that, but small museums and collections are likely to be run by volunteers. Typically, understaffed, undertrained, overwhelmed with work, and low on funds."

"How are the sales handled?" Surely, one didn't buy online or pay with a credit card.

"Generally, through private auctions," he said. "Notices of sales go to particular possible bidders. You have to know the right people to get in."

"Really?" My eyebrows shot up. "Like a Sotheby's run by thugs?"

"Between you and me, they could be doing it at Sotheby's. In fact, there's a case involving Sotheby's. But for the most part, they do it online, in a secured chat room. I don't know all the particulars, but smuggling and black market transactions have gone digital. A computer expert would know more about the technical aspects." Kirov paused and gazed out the window. "Oh, brave new world," he intoned. His expression grew wistful.

"No kidding," I said, scribbling notes.

Kirov turned back to me. "You asked about ownership. Sometimes valuable items can be found in someone's attic or other places." He made air quotes around the word "found." "In those cases," he continued. "it's handy if someone completely legit on the surface finds the item."

"You mean, to act as a front," I said.

"Yes. Exactly."

This raised all sorts of interesting possibilities. Kandinsky could have been killed for just about any reason. But the fact that he hung out at the art school made me wonder. Could his death have been connected in any way to the disappearance of

Blaine's daughter? Could Kandinsky have been working with someone at MICA to help sell smuggled artifacts?

"I would love to get your opinion on this," I said. "How likely would it be for an artist to deal in smuggled artifacts?"

Kirov raised an eyebrow. "I wouldn't assume anything about that. Anyone interested in making money could be involved in smuggling."

"But would an artist be considered a good front?"

"That would depend on the artist, I think." He paused, and then said, "It's a matter of reputation. There are lawyers, doctors, and others who have the credibility to act as a front."

I nodded. "So a businessman who's a patron of the arts might count? Or an artist who benefits from one?"

"Sure." Kirov turned his hands palm up in a "why not" gesture.

"Thank you, Doctor Kirov."

"Please. Call me George."

"Thank you, George. Call me Erica. If you can think of anything else that might help, please call me." I delved into my bag, pulled out my card, and handed it to him.

I left the building, eager to update my notes. Instead of heading straight to my car, I stopped at one of the campus libraries where I chose a table with enough space to spread out my notes and diagram. I drew more lines between various possible players. Next to MICA, I put a question mark. Could someone at MICA be involved?

By the time I finished, it was well past noon and I was getting hungry. I thought of hitting a deli or some other kind of eatery nearby. On the way out, I noticed an actual coffee shop, right in the library. I wandered inside, where my gaze lit upon a display case of muffins and other pastries. Tempting, but on the pricey side. I decided to take my chances on a Route 1 fast-food joint.

I hiked back to the car and fired it up. I eased out of the space and made a quick left toward the campus exit. I hit the brake as I approached the exit intersection. The pedal felt mushy, but the car slowed enough to turn onto University Boulevard. As I came up to the interchange at Route 1 and University Boulevard, I pressed the brake again. Nothing happened. I hit the pedal hard, but the car refused to slow. The Fiesta had to be doing around 45 or 50 miles per hour. That got the adrenaline going.

Shit.

CHAPTER THIRTEEN

My foot mashed the brake, but the car barreled on. Automatically, I slammed the pedal again. Nothing. By then, I was into a wide turn sweeping right onto a connecting road that led to Route 1.

The weird thing about post-traumatic stress is that it affects you in the oddest ways, at the least expected times. Instead of panicking, my instincts kicked in, and a surreal calm settled over me.

To make the turn, I wrested the wheel to the right. The car's left side skidded onto the shoulder, but the right side tires gripped the pavement. I managed to reach the connecting road, and my car tore on in the right lane. I couldn't imagine making it to Route 1 without plowing into a phone pole or another vehicle.

I sideswiped the tires against the curb, which did little more than ruin good tires. Slowly, I pulled the handbrake. The car slowed a bit, so I pulled harder. The car shuddered to a halt curbside a few feet short of the intersection.

Exhaling a breath, I stared through the windshield. After a minute, I hit my four-way flashers and called AAA.

φφφ

The AAA tow truck took nearly an hour to arrive. But that gave me plenty of time to figure out my next move. Sure, my car was old, but I kept up regular maintenance. Perhaps the brake line had sprung a leak when I hit a pothole or had accidentally run over something.

Or had the brake been monkeyed with. Who would do it? Who knew I'd be at the university that day? I hadn't told Terry my exact plans. Maybe someone who knew him found out. Surely, it wasn't the guys he'd expected to greet with his gun in hand. I called Two-Bit Terry and got his voice mail.

I mulled over these questions as I rode with the tow truck driver, who seemed hell-bent on engaging me in conversation.

"Sorry I took so long," he said. The driver wore washed-out denim overalls (bib and all) over a red-and-white checkered shirt. Looked like he should've been driving a farm tractor.

"No problem."

"Leastwise, it's not raining or snowing, huh?"

"Right. Snow in September would be weird."

The driver laughed, taking my comment as an invitation to keep talking. Someday, I'll learn to keep my mouth shut.

"Well, with that global warming stuff going on, you never know what the weather will be, right?" he said.

"Yeah." Full stop.

He chuckled and shook his head. "That's quite a car you have there. Fiesta Mark I, right? Cute little things."

"It runs."

"Haven't seen a Mark I in ages," he continued. "German-built, but the ones sold here had more kick than the overseas models."

I smiled, despite myself. "Really?"

"I love working on cars. 'Specially old ones." His gaze through the windshield turned wistful. "Done my share of engine and body restoration. You know, people don't hold onto things like they used to. Everyone's chasing what's shiny and new." He glanced my way. "Name's Clyde Beavers. You ever need work done on your car, I'm a mechanic on the side."

"That's nice."

"I don't charge an arm and a leg, neither. Too many folks in this line look to gouge customers. Especially when they're—no offense, miss—women."

I turned to look him over. Seemed like a decent guy. "Got a card?"

"Sure thing. The wife just ran a load off for me. Got 'em right here." He reached into a pocket in the bib of his overalls and handed me a white card with a name and contact information printed on it. He lived not far from me.

"Thanks," I said, tucking the card into my bag. "And I'm Erica," I added, passing him one of mine.

When we arrived at the shop, I thanked him once more and gave him a $10 tip before exiting the tow truck. Good thing I hadn't stopped at the Overpriced Cafe. In the meantime, a bag of overly-salty chips from a vending machine would have to be my lunch while I waited for the vehicular verdict.

I returned to pondering my situation as the mechanic examined my car. Two other customers sat with me in the waiting room. A small TV set perched above us blared an annoying talk show. If I had to spend hours listening to mindless chatter on that TV, I'd probably smash it with my chair.

A thin young man wearing a light blue shirt and dark blue slacks, identified as "Roy" on an oval embroidered name tag, emerged from the shop area, wiping his hands on a greasy rag. "Ms. Jensen?" His eyes scanned the group.

"Here." I raised my hand like an elementary school student.

"Follow me, please." He crooked his finger, and I trailed him toward my car.

My car was still on the lift, and Roy beckoned for me to follow him underneath it. With the hope that it wouldn't come crashing down, I gingerly ducked under the vehicle.

"See that?" Roy pointed a smudged finger toward what I assumed was the brake line, unblemished and completely intact. "That's the replacement. Now here's what I took out."

He waved me over to a workbench strewn with tools and replacement parts. The young man plucked an identical, but dirty line from the disarray. It was smooth, except for the small break in the line.

"This line was in good shape," he said. "Your leak wasn't caused by a faulty line. You ask me, I'd say it was vandalism."

φφφ

I didn't bother calling the cops. What would they do? Automobile vandalism wasn't exactly a high-priority crime.

At least I knew I had someone's attention. The questions were Why? and Who? Was it because I'd followed up on finding Kandinsky's body or my inquiries about Melissa? Were they connected?

As I drove home from the shop, I kept a lookout for suspicious cars or people. I felt the vague tingle under my skin that came when I thought I was being watched, a side effect of my time in Afghanistan. I had something of a sixth sense when it came to trouble.

So it wasn't a huge shock when I realized that a brown SUV a few cars behind me had been on my tail several miles after I'd left the garage. I slid over two lanes to the right and swung onto a residential side road. Doing a quick scan, I noted few hiding places. Except for one well-placed line of juniper bushes. I pulled my car over, jumped out and scurried behind the hedge. The brown SUV slowed, then sped up to pass. But not before I got a photo of the license plate.

CHAPTER FOURTEEN

I returned to my home office and logged into one of my databases. A quick search on the license plate number revealed the SUV's owner was a guy named Brian Weis. According to the file, Weis lived in Baltimore, mere blocks from MICA. I jotted down the address and added another name to my diagram. The nature of his connection to be determined.

φφφ

When I arrived in Weis' neighborhood, I deliberately drove past the street he lived on. For one thing, the curb was jammed with cars. For another, I wanted to be as inconspicuous as possible. If Weis had cut my brake line, parking too close to his residence would be asking for trouble.

The neighborhood was typical West Baltimore. Stone or brick rowhouses with marble steps at the entrances, some with Victorian-like facades that had lots of curlicues and scalloped trim.

I spied a parking space just big enough for my Fiesta. One benefit of driving a small car—it's much easier to hide than a big honkin' SUV.

After parking, I strolled toward Weis' address. My plan was to scope out the house, find a spot for surveillance, and move the car closer to it, if possible. I had no intention of knocking on the front door. Most urban residences have peepholes. If Weis was home, what were the chances he would look through the peephole and decide not to open the door to me? I live in the suburbs and don't open my door without first doing a rudimentary check.

When I reached the intersection with Weis' street, I didn't immediately see the SUV. Maybe he wasn't home or maybe he'd parked farther from his house, which was two doors from the intersection, where I stood catty-corner. I crossed Weis's street and continued straight, until I reached an alley that extended both ways behind a long line of buildings, Weis' stone rowhouse included. I spotted the SUV parked behind his house.

The Fiesta could fit in the small space between the street and a dumpster on my side of the alley, which provided a fine view of the SUV. I didn't see any "No Parking" signs, so I boogied back to my car and motored to the space. I backed in, hoping no one would hassle me.

In the interest of making sure it was the same SUV, I got out of my car and walked toward the vehicle to get a closer look. The license plate matched, so I inched closer to get a quick peek through the back window. There were several crates piled up in the storage area. Interesting. I snapped a photo.

The sound of a door opening and footsteps meant that I needed to move away, so I quickly scanned the area for a hiding place. The footsteps grew louder. I hustled behind another dumpster.

From my hiding place, I saw a man open the back of the SUV. He moved out of view and returned with another crate, which he heaved into the vehicle. He looked to be my age or maybe younger. Rail thin, with scruffy brown hair and the hint of a goatee. I snapped another photo.

Moving toward the man, I said, "Brian Weis?"

The man peered at me. "Who's asking?"

I extended my hand. "The woman whose car you followed earlier today. Nice to meet you."

Weis looked nonplussed. "Huh?"

"I looked up your license plate," I said. "Or, wait . . . let me guess. Someone borrowed your SUV?"

"No," he declared. "And I got no idea what you're talking about."

Oh, a cool customer. What fun.

"What's in those crates?" I asked, gesturing toward the vehicle.

"Nothing." He turned away.

"So, if I tell the police that an SUV with your license plate followed me after my car was vandalized, that wouldn't be a problem for you? Since you know so little about it."

He paused, but wouldn't make eye contact. "Do what you want," Weis retorted over his shoulder as he went back into the house.

I intended to do just that. I ducked beside the SUV, where Weis couldn't see me from the house and fished an old set of lock picks from my shoulder bag. I hurried toward the back of the vehicle and jimmied open the door's lock. Just plain, white boxes. No markings. My gaze shifting from the house to the boxes, I threw off one of the lids. The close-up shots of what lay inside were well worth the profanities from Weis when he burst out the back door, and after one short second of sizing up the situation, started after me as fast as he could run.

CHAPTER FIFTEEN

The sound of Weis charging out of his back door gave me just the surge of energy I needed to get away. I pounded down the alley away from the vehicle, with him hot on my trail and shouting at the top of his lungs.

When does a Marine run from a fight? When she's on probation and in anger management therapy. But don't get me wrong. Frankly, I ran because I was afraid I would break Weis' neck if we got into a fight.

I hadn't come with the intent to fight the guy. The last thing I needed was an assault and battery charge on top of everything else.

Rounding the corner, I scanned the street and bolted into a convenience store three doors down. From behind a shelf of chips and cookies, I peered through the plate glass front. Weis came into view and I ducked, which set off a painful twinge in my back. Great.

Bending low to avoid being seen by Weis, I ignored the pain and crept toward the rear of the store. A short, swarthy man with a pickle-shaped nose eyed the shelves and scribbled on a clipboard.

"Excuse me," I mumbled, feeling ridiculous.

Pickle Nose gave me a curious look.

"Is there a back door?" I asked, with as much desperation as I could. I jerked a thumb toward the window. "That man outside is stalking me."

The man looked like a Middle Easterner, and for that reason, I figured he probably understood what being harassed was like.

After the quickest glance out the window, Pickle Nose nodded. He gestured for me to follow him into the back. Just in time, as it happened, since Weis chose that moment to enter.

The man guided me to an exit that opened into yet another alley.

"Thank you," I said.

He nodded, moving his hands about. "No problem."

If only there'd been more of you in Afghanistan, I thought. And then appended that with, *and whose fault was that?*

I checked both directions, but I couldn't tell exactly where I was vis-à-vis my car. My gut told me to go left.

I checked my surroundings at the intersection. It seemed this alley led me to a point about half a block from my car. With the hope that the man at the convenience store was keeping Weis occupied, I made tracks toward my car. A glance back revealed no sign of my quarry as I approached my car.

Once safely inside, I pulled my car behind the dumpster, to make it invisible from the street but still in a good place to maintain surveillance using the right side rear-view mirror. I slouched in my seat and waited. While I was waiting, I used up a bit of my precious data to email the photos to myself . . . just in case I lost my phone. Pictures of metal icons and crucifixes engraved with intricate patterns. If those weren't pictures of valuable artifacts, I'd eat my external hard drive.

It wasn't long before Weis plodded into view. He seemed grumpy, even from a distance. Not that I could blame him. But part of me savored the feeling of escape. *Amateur*, I thought.

Weis meandered home and reentered the house. I moved the car back to the spot near the street. Ignoring the pain in my lower spine, I settled in for a wait. I assumed that Weis was loading the SUV with the intent of taking its precious cargo somewhere. When he left, I would follow. *Turnabout is fair play.*

I kept my eye on the SUV while scanning the periphery. Maintaining a constant state of awareness came easily to me now . . . a little too easily sometimes.

Unfortunately, even the best laid plans sometimes fall apart. Like the moment I saw Weis leave his house and walk toward the nearest intersection. He waited to cross the street.

I left my car and hugged the opposite wall, where I could check Weis' progress without being seen. He crossed to my side of the road and disappeared behind the building. I hustled toward the corner and cautiously peeked around it to see Weis walking really fast, now almost a block away. I followed, trying to look nonchalant while keeping an eye on him.

I could only hope he wouldn't look back and recognize me. If I were a "real private eye," I might have come better equipped to follow people out in public. Alas . . . I didn't arm myself with a bag full of wigs or even a hat. Then, I wondered if actual private eyes really did that anymore. Or ever.

I pulled a pair of sunglasses out of my shoulder bag, which I donned in a somewhat lame attempt to avoid being recognized. Weis seemed hell bent on getting somewhere fast, which gave me hope that he wouldn't turn around.

Weis reached another intersection and made a left. Scrambling to catch up, I stopped short of the edge of the building, leaned against it, and did a quick visual sweep. Half a block away, Weis was climbing steps flanked by wrought iron rails adorned with distinctive curlicues. He fished a key from his pocket, but entered the building without using it.

Interesting, I thought. His parents' place? Or someone else's? An apartment in this building would make an expensive storage space.

As I approached the building, I reflexively scanned for hiding places and emergency escape routes. From what I'd seen, it appeared that the building had an unlocked entryway, which would suggest the residents lived in apartments or condos. Not knowing whether Weis's destination faced the street or not put me at a disadvantage. Nonetheless, I was too curious to turn back.

Mounting the steps, I entered what turned out to be a small vestibule with a locked door providing access to the rest of the building. A door through which my quarry had disappeared.

The wall to my right was lined with mailboxes. A phone was mounted on the wall next to them. A quick check of the mailboxes revealed . . . nothing.

Great.

CHAPTER SIXTEEN

The way I saw it, I had two choices: hang around for God knew how long waiting for Weis or move on and save him for later. For all I knew, Weis could have left already through a back door. I went back out and maneuvered through the alleys in an impromptu recon mission around the building. Didn't see anything and didn't figure on it.

Since I was near the art school, taking my photos there and seeking an artifacts expert seemed the better course of action. As for my throbbing back, I'd power through it.

I returned to my car and thought about Melissa Blaine's situation as I drove toward MICA. Finding her would clearly take more than the three hours Blaine and I had agreed upon. This was assuming her disappearance wasn't connected to Kandinsky's death and/or the artifacts in Weis' SUV.

En route to the school, it hit me. Ancient artifacts are not only the purview of art experts. I'd probably need to run the photos by a museum curator, if not an archaeologist. And who knew how much they could glean from photos snapped on a cell phone?

I turned onto a side street and pulled into the first spot I saw. Once again, I tried to reach Two-Bit Terry and got his voicemail. My message was short and prefaced with a long sigh. "Erica again. Please call me."

Time to review my options. I pulled out my makeshift flowchart and eyed it looking for previously unseen connections. A glance at Google Maps showed a few museums in the Baltimore area, but I considered taking a trip to D.C. where the Mother of all American Museums—the Smithsonian—had its headquarters.

The phone trilled. My eager gaze locked on the caller ID, only to find that it wasn't Terry. But the number did ring a bell. After a moment's consideration, I answered.

"Erica? Hi, it's Nick Baxter."

Nick Baxter? I pulled a momentary blank.

"From the support group," he added.

Oh.

"The journalist?" I said.

"Right," he answered. "The unemployed journalist."

"The word is freelancer."

"Yeah or consultant. I've heard all the jokes." His voice was weary. "I wanted to see if you'd like to meet for coffee sometime," he added. There was an inkling of suppressed hope in his voice.

That depends, I thought. Is this really about meeting for coffee or more? Don't get me wrong. He seemed like a nice enough guy. And I could go for the coffee or even a chat with a journalist (unemployed or otherwise), but not much more. Depending on what "more" entailed.

"Wait, let me check my busy social schedule," I said. Half a second later, I added, "Well, what do you know? I can meet you now."

"I'm in D.C."

"I'm in Baltimore."

He laughed. I smiled. "How about we split the difference and meet in Laurel. Have you been to More Than Java Café on Main Street?"

"I know it. See you there in, say, half an hour?"

φφφ

Thirty-five minutes later, Nick and I sipped our coffees at one of the tables by a window. After the usual polite chitchat, Nick said, "I actually hoped to ask you . . . " A thin line between his eyes deepened.

To marry me? A sarcastic response that went unspoken.

Nick's expression smoothed. "I'm looking for a sponsor. Would you consider it?" The words rushed out of his mouth as if propelled by a gust of wind.

I cradled my coffee cup in both hands. "That depends." I leaned toward him, keeping my voice low. "Can I tell you something that's specifically not for publication?"

He nodded. "Of course."

I drew closer and murmured, "Would you be interested in assisting an unlicensed private eye, who wants to go legit?"

CHAPTER SEVENTEEN

For a moment, Nick stared at me. It was an elastic moment that seemed to stretch way out.

"You mean—," he started.

"Yes, I mean me." I smiled with all requisite enthusiasm. "You asked what I did. Now you know."

Nick sipped his coffee. "Why are you unlicensed?"

"Want the long version or the short?"

He studied my face. "Whatever you feel comfortable sharing."

"Okay, here's a short one." I took another swig from my cup, taking time to decide on where to begin. "I'm a Marine. Between concussions, lower back pain from the weight of my protective armor, and a case of PTSD, I became addicted to the painkillers my doctors prescribed.

"Because my medical treatment comes through the VA, my addiction is a matter of military record. In Maryland, anyone addicted to narcotics is disqualified from obtaining an official investigator's license. I don't dare lie about this on an application. Being addicted is bad enough."

I let the words hang. I stared into my coffee cup.

When I raised my glance, he was nodding, sympathy in his eyes.

"I was embedded with a platoon in Iraq," he said. He convulsed in a brief shiver. "I'll never forget what I heard and saw there. I don't have to tell you it wasn't pretty."

"Mmm." What could I say? "Is that how you . . . ?"

"Became an addict?" He shook his head. "Between the memories and the mass layoffs, I went off the rails."

Derailed. Great description of my life. Our lives.

"So . . . you want me as your sponsor?" My tone betrayed my disbelief.

"Yes, please," Nick said. "I'll be glad to help you in return, as long as it's nothing illegal."

"No worries," I assured him. "I need help finding resources and developing contacts. Usually, this isn't a problem. Up until recently, my job has been limited to discovering assets. But now, I'm now handling a matter that involves questioning people. Frankly, my people skills are rusty. As a journalist, I suspect you're much better at dealing with other people than I am."

"And I have contacts," he added.

"Just what I hoped you would say."

I dug out my cell phone and displayed the artifact photos. "Check these out. I have no idea if anyone can authenticate them as obscure Georgian artifacts from a photo, but I wouldn't mind having an expert look at them."

Nick accepted the cell phone from my extended hand and inspected the images. "Not exactly my former beat, but I know another reporter who might know someone. I'll give her a call."

He took out his phone, punched some buttons, and, apparently, reached the source. Without going into a lot of detail, Nick said he was looking for a Soviet artifacts expert. The response seemed to please him. He pulled out a small notepad and pen, then made a hasty looping scrawl across the pad.

"Thanks. I owe you," he said, before disconnecting.

Nick pushed the notepad toward me. "A retired Russian archeologist who came here shortly after the Wall fell. The Berlin Wall."

"I know my history," I snapped. Oops. Rude. "I mean, thanks."

"No problem," he assured me.

I scanned the scrawled note, and the name Dr. Peter Amelin emerged from the looping handwriting, along with a number I could just barely make out.

"Are you still sure you want me as a sponsor?" I asked.

He nodded. "Do me a favor. Go into your recent calls."

So I did. "Save your number?" I guessed.

"Exactly," he said. "Now I have your number and you have mine."

CHAPTER EIGHTEEN

Nick and I parted ways with mutual promises to stay in touch. The thought of having an unofficial partner or mentor was unfamiliar. I hadn't had to work alongside anyone since my time with the FET. Surely, working with me in the United States couldn't be as potentially deadly as doing that in a war zone.

Before I left Laurel, I called Peter Amelin. He answered on the third ring with a heavily accented "Hello."

I introduced myself and explained the problem, leaving out most of the worrisome details. "Would you be able to determine anything about an object's authenticity from a cellphone photo?"

"Hmmm." It was the lowest C possible on a pipe organ. "In the strictest sense, I can't really authenticate objects from a photo. I would need to use spectroscopic analysis for that. But I could look at the photos and judge whether they have the outward appearance of Svaneti artifacts. It won't tell you much, but I can do that."

"That would be great," I said. "Could we meet today?"

He gave me his address and invited me to come by in an hour or so.

φφφ

Amelin lived in a brick rambler, not unlike the many brick ramblers on one of the side streets off Randolph Road where it passed Wheaton High School. Passing Wheaton High always made me think of Joan Jett, because she'd gone to school there. Then, she moved to California. Good for Joan.

Amelin's brick rambler had a small front yard with a tall maple tree that had yet to turn color and a row of azalea bushes that weren't in bloom because it was September. It also had the kind of fancy front walk that you get from a landscape architect—an arrangement of irregular-shaped flat stones in a line that curved toward the door. I stepped carefully from stone to stone and managed to make it to the front door without tripping.

Despite the familiarity and quiet of the neighborhood, I felt a nervous tickle in my subconscious that made me itch all over.

One ring of the doorbell and Amelin was there within moments. "Ms. Jensen?" He extended a smooth hand with unusually long fingers—the immaculate hand of a scholar. "It's nice to meet you."

"Thanks for inviting me, Dr. Amelin," I said. "And please call me Erica."

He waved me in. "Then you must call me Peter. Please." Again, the hand waved his permission to enter.

He closed the door behind me and led me from the small foyer into a comfortable living room, furnished in soft grays and blues. It was a living room that merited the name, because it actually looked lived in.

"Tea? Coffee?" he asked.

"No, thanks. This won't take long."

Amelin sat on a blue-gray sofa, which was perpendicular to a matching love seat. I took my place on the end of the love seat nearest him—my cell phone in hand. I put on a smile. Lord knew, I could use the practice.

"I appreciate your taking the time for this," I said, adding, "Peter."

Amelin grinned as if I'd said the funniest thing. "Let's take a look at those photos, eh?"

I brought up the pictures and swiped through them while he watched.

"Hold on," he said, raising his hand. "Two shots back. I'd like a closer look at that one."

I displayed the photo in question and handed him the phone. Amelin peered at the screen. He placed the phone on a small side table at the intersection of our seating.

"One moment, please." Amelin opened a drawer in the side table and retrieved what looked like a photographer's loupe. He picked up the phone again, enlarged the image, eyeballed it, then observed it through the loupe. As he gazed at the photo, I shifted in my seat to keep my back from barking at me.

Finally, Amelin shook his head. "I cannot give a firm opinion on the authenticity of these. But even if they are not real, they might convince an amateur."

"What is it about them that makes you think they might be real?" I asked.

Amelin replaced the phone on the little table. "Excuse me," he said. He rose and left the room. I stared at the photo, then looked around the room and ran my hand along the love seat's cushion. Silky, almost. It was a nice, middle-class room, furnished with an impressionist oil painting and pieces that might have belonged to my grandparents. I continued looking for ways to distract myself from the pain in my back until Amelin returned. He had a magazine in hand, opened to a specific page.

"I collect some of these," he said, holding up the magazine. "A publication for archaeologists and artifacts experts. Occasionally, they feature a subject in my particular field."

He sat down again and showed me the page. "Now, these are actual artifacts recovered by authorities who were investigating a smuggling ring." Amelin handed the magazine to me.

I checked the photo and compared it with my cell phone pictures. I could see what he meant. The resemblance between them was clear.

"So what do you see that suggests they might be fake?" I asked.

Amelin gave me the "aren't you funny" grin again. "It is not a matter of how they look. There is money to be made in selling fake artifacts."

"So, it's just a possibility."

"A distinct possibility." He raised his finger in a professorial manner. "Had you ever heard of Svaneti before?"

"A friend told me about it. It relates to another matter." *And let's not go there.*

"How likely is it that anyone would have ready access to genuine artifacts from a place like that?" Amelin queried.

"Not likely, unless they knew someone. Had an inside connection."

"There is your answer," he said. "You must find that connection to know whether these are genuine or not."

CHAPTER NINETEEN

After talking to Amelin, I sat in my car and reviewed my jottings. I combined what I had learned from him with what I'd learned before our meeting. None of it gave me any comfort.

The scenario Blaine had presented—one in which Kandinsky might have skimmed a portion of the partnership's profits—was metastasizing into something much worse—a phony artifacts smuggling ring. But I couldn't know for sure without poking my nose where it might get cut off.

If Kandinsky had been part of a smuggling ring and the artifacts were fakes, that could explain why he was murdered. Or he might have been killed by a jealous competitor. Maybe Kandinsky's death had nothing to do with either of those things.

The problem is, I don't believe in coincidences. I doubted that I had simply stumbled across Kandinsky's body, met with an art instructor and a criminologist, and then become the random victim of a passing vandal with time on his hands (and a sharp knife) who cut my brake line.

I went home and turned my attention to other work that was waiting for me—small-change stuff, but clients, nonetheless. While I was at the computer, I tried again to find information about Melissa Blaine—free information, that is. Once again, I came up almost empty handed. I did happen across a Web site that featured artwork credited to "Melissa B." Very nice, but not very helpful. I wondered how she managed to keep such a low online profile.

That night, I decided to read a book to relax before hitting the sack . . . but I was still haunted by the nightmares.

φφφ

A car is approaching the outpost. I motion for it to stop, but it keeps coming. My partner yells at the driver. We both yell and gesture, but that doesn't change a thing.

This damn place is so hot, it's like an oven. I squint against the glare of the sun and the grit of sand blowing against my face. Focus on the dark object barreling towards us out of the white heat. Why won't it stop?

Screaming the word "halt" over and over seems ridiculous. Does the driver even speak English? By now, you would think they'd have learned what the word meant, though. Surely they understand my frantic motions.

My partner raises his M16, sites the oncoming vehicle through its ACOG Riflescope. Almost simultaneously, I do the same. We're synchronized, like we're on parade. Or a perverse new Olympic event. Our drill sergeant from boot camp would be impressed.

My mouth is dry and my heart pounds. No time for thinking or feeling. I'm a Marine. This is what we do. Aim and shoot. Protect and defend. Kill.

The car is almost on us when I pull the trigger. I aim for a tire. Shots ring out. The sound echoes as a child runs toward me. The scene has changed. I'm on a street in Kandahar, in the middle of a neighborhood in ruins. Hot as hell, positioned behind a fallen wall, laboring under the weight of pounds of gear not designed for my body, but rifle at the ready.

The child reaches me—a small boy. He's crying. I give him a one-armed hug, checking to see if some joker has strapped a bomb to this kid. All good. When I return to my position, the boy's tears have turned to blood. The boom of an explosion knocks me to the ground. Knocks the wind out of me. For a moment, I'm too dizzy to move.

When I look up, the boy still stands there. He's stopped crying. But the blood is all over his face. Oozing from his pores like sweat.

I try to speak to him, but no words come. How can he still be standing, bleeding from every pore? I see it on his arms now.

I don't understand. But the boy stares at me, without blinking. Then I realize he's dead as another explosion topples him in front of me.

And, not for the first time, I realize that death is just inches away from me.

Now, I'm in the mine-resistant vehicle with Perkins. He drives. I'm beside him—M16 at the ready. An electric jolt runs up my back as the vehicle bounces down the dusty road. If you can dignify the narrow strip of ground as such. The strip of ground is packed sand, the same relentless dusty beige as its surroundings.

We're on our way home. Then, an explosion, and everything turns black.

φφφ

I jolt awake after the explosion. I am drenched in sweat. Gasping for air. My heart pounds to the same beat I feel in my head.

What I wouldn't give for a single night of peaceful dreams. Reluctantly, I get out of bed and force myself to face another day.

CHAPTER TWENTY

I toss my nightshirt aside and wander toward the bathroom like a zombie. Brush teeth, step into the shower. The water washes the sweat away, but my anxiety is still there.

As I go through the motions of making a minimal breakfast, my thoughts churn. The past few days' events flash by in my head. I need to write them down—and use what I've learned to somehow connect the players on my flowchart.

I force myself to meditate for ten minutes, then do my yoga stretches. To my astonishment, it helps. A little.

I suddenly remember that I still haven't heard back from Terry. Time to check up on him.

φφφ

On the way to Terry's apartment, I tried to figure out why he hadn't returned my calls. Maybe he lost his phone or maybe it died, but I didn't really believe either one. Of course, anything was possible, but there was only one way to find out.

I backed into a space outside Terry's building and started to walk toward the entrance. His car was parked several spaces from mine. A glance at a small opening in his mailbox revealed that he hadn't retrieved his mail. There were times when I could go for days without checking my own mail and not regret it, but I had to empty the box sooner or later. In any case, seeing a full mailbox was a little unnerving, considering that Terry had failed to return my calls or text me.

I climbed the steps and gave his door three sharp raps. No response. More rapping produced more nothing. I tried the knob. Locked. I sighed and dug through my shoulder bag for my handy-dandy bump key.

As I wrestled with the key, I kept my ears open and occasionally looked over my shoulder to make sure no one was sneaking up on me. The itchy feeling I had developed felt like a case of poison ivy—internal.

After what seemed like eons of whacking on the key with one hand and adjusting its placement with the other, the door lock finally gave way. I opened the door very slowly. My overly cautious entrée into Terry's apartment was unrewarded. Not a soul in sight. No Terry. No strangers who might be disgruntled hackers or whatever else.

I eased inside and shut the door behind me. After the soft click of the door closing, I sensed an eerie hush about the place . . . not a sound from within or without. The neighbors must be at work. Then I heard a faint *squeak squeak* from above. The upstairs neighbor was home. Or being robbed by the world's dumbest burglar. Not my business.

"Terry." The word slipped out, not loudly, but loud enough to be heard in the unusual silence. Moving through the small apartment, I could see that nothing had been disturbed. The furniture, the closets, the kitchen, the bathroom—it all looked unmolested by intruders. Terry's toothbrush was in its holder. Maybe he'd taken an impromptu trip and forgotten it.

I checked the fridge again. Nothing much in it, except for a few essentials. Condiments, jam, nothing that would spoil. Except for the take-out Chinese food shoved to the back. Thought about smelling it and changed my mind.

In the freezer, I found a stack of frozen foods. Those meal-in-a-box deals. This was Terry's diet. Frozen dinners, take-out, and condiments. The booze was probably under the sink.

Now for a list of things I did not find. I did not find a flight itinerary, credit card statements, old letters, a note written in invisible ink, a message hastily scrawled on the wall in blood, or any of those other fool things that invariably make their way into detective stories.

I also didn't find Terry's dead body. That was the good news.

I took one last look beneath furniture, behind a calendar, inside drawers and in every other conceivable hiding place. Under the bed, I saw what seemed like a dark lump of some kind. A closer look revealed a rectangular shape. I swept an arm beneath the bed frame and managed to snag it.

It was a cell phone. A cursory inspection made it clear it was Terry's and out of juice.

What was Terry's cell phone doing under the bed?

CHAPTER TWENTY-ONE

The find sickened me. Terry wouldn't have left willingly without his phone. I saw no sign of a fight. Not unless they had a knock-down drag out and straightened up afterward—highly doubtful.

But the phone could have been kicked under the bed. Possibly by someone holding a gun on Terry. And if this had anything to do with my inquiries into the Georgian (or Svanetian) letter, then it could be my fault that Terry was . . . Kidnapped? Being tortured? Dead?

I tried to shut down this new train of thought, which was sheer supposition anyway. Maybe the hackers coming after him were angry enough to take him hostage. But without any struggle from Terry? Nah.

The police. I should file a missing persons report. Tell them everything I'd had done to try to reach Terry. I would leave out the part about breaking into his apartment. They could search it for themselves if they wanted to.

It was the least I could do if Blaine's case related to Terry's disappearance. And, at this point, the least I could do was the best I could do.

φφφ

After exhausting every possible hiding place for clues, I left Terry's apartment. My spidey-sense tingled. The internal poison ivy flared. That too-familiar feeling of bad vibes from my time being deployed overseas. As I walked to my car, I felt a presence behind me. The presence walked quietly as a cat, but his footsteps whispered against the pavement in a way that told me he was large and heavy. I say "he", because I caught a glimpse of his shadow. It could've been Sasquatch's.

"Excuse me," a voice rumbled at my back. I stopped and turned. A man approached me. He was like a gorilla, with possibly a bit less hair.

The lights went out for a moment. Then, I realized the man was on the ground, out cold. I felt slightly dizzy, but remained upright. My arms ached a bit. They felt like I'd been lifting weights.

A blackout. I hadn't had one in ages. But then I hadn't felt this threatened in a long time.

Itchiness swept through me. Bugs crawled up my spine. I scanned the surrounding buildings. Saw a glimmer on the roof. I dove for the pavement, trying to keep my chin from scraping concrete, but not quite succeeding.

Zzzip. Crack. The sounds verified my fears. The bullet grazed the nearby shrubbery, thudding into the ground. Too close.

I pushed myself up with caution, looking toward where light had reflected off the sniper's scope. Nothing there. I touched my chin. Blood stained my hand. Facial wounds always seem worse than they are, blood-wise, but I needed to staunch the flow before I dripped all over one of my few decent shirts.

The Gorilla Man stirred, his eyes still shut. *Time to leave.* I forced myself to stand and made a wobbly-legged run for the car.

CHAPTER TWENTY-TWO

I managed to start the car and pull out of the lot without getting shot at a second time, which was a step in the right direction. Now, I needed to figure out what in God's name to do next.

My mind spun with possibilities. *Focus, focus, focus*—my current mantra.

My first thought was to go to the cops. And not just to report what I saw in Terry's apartment. There was the failure to contact him, the uncharged phone under the bed, plus a sniper taking shots at me in full daylight. It had to be someone staking Terry's place out. If so, why had Gorilla Man not followed me inside? Could Gorilla Man have been looking for Terry, too? His interest in me might have been completely benign.

That's the thing about PTSD. Your senses become too acute. Even a person's shadow made me jumpy. And for all I knew, he might have had no connection to the sniper.

Did any of this have anything to do with my work for Blaine? Or ancient artifacts that might've been smuggled from Soviet Georgia (or some part thereof)?

As I drove away, my gaze darted from the rearview mirror to the road. No sign of anyone following me.

A mile or two down the road, I turned onto a side street and pulled over. I retrieved the notepad from my file and wrote down everything I remembered of the incident. If I went to the cops, they'd want a statement. Writing it now would keep the details fresh.

I felt my back twinge again. With all the excitement, adrenaline had masked the return of that blasted backache.

I considered my options. If I went to the police, what could they do if the Mob was involved? We hadn't had any serial sniper shootings in the area since 2002 when two snipers terrorized the whole DC area and beyond. And despite my concern about Terry, how likely were the cops to make any effort to find him? Was it worth defying my wealthy client's wishes to keep the police out of it?

But then there was Melissa. Did she fit into this picture anywhere? I'd already put in my three hours toward finding her and then some. But now my friend was missing, too. And the sniper made it clear that the Mob or someone wasn't just screwing around.

I knew for sure that something was off. I knew from my time in the Corps that a good sniper could have taken me out. If the intent was to kill me, I'd be dead.

One thing was clear. It was time for another meet with the client. We needed to get a few things straight.

φφφ

Blaine answered on the second ring with an abrupt, "Yes?"

"We need to meet as soon as possible," I said.

"Why? Any news about my daughter?"

"I haven't found her, but there are matters I need to discuss with you."

"So discuss," he snapped. "What's going on?"

"Not on the phone," I insisted. "We need to talk face-to-face."

The sound from the other end could have been either a groan or a growl. "I don't have time to waste on meetings. Talk to me."

Fine. "To put it in a nutshell, I haven't found your daughter or your money. Your partner, as you know, is . . . no longer with us. But I've come to believe that he may have been involved in an illegal activity. Your money may have gone toward that. To date, my car's brakes have been tampered with, I've been followed, and someone took a shot at me. Either you meet with me to talk about this or I go to the police."

Blaine's grunt was dismissive. "Then let me put your mind at ease. You're fired."

Ah, how different the rich are from you and me. "Mr. Blaine. Stuart," I said. "Hear me out."

Wasted words. Blaine had hung up.

CHAPTER TWENTY-THREE

"Fantastic," I said, as I disconnected and stowed the phone. So much for that client. So much for this month's rent money. Now what?

I reviewed the situation. What did I owe Blaine other than a refund—partial refund? He'd tossed me aside like a pair of old shoes. That left me with the decision about the police.

If I blabbed to the cops about the ins and outs of my relationship with Blaine, would it affect my reputation as a licensed private eye somewhere down the road? But there was more at stake than Blaine's problems. Apart from the fact that I'd been shot at by someone keeping surveillance on Terry's apartment, there was the unsettling matter of Terry's disappearance.

My head throbbed, my back ached, and my chin stung where it had kissed the sidewalk. I angled the rearview mirror for a look at the damage. Minor road rash. I'd suffered worse.

"The hell with it," I announced to no one in particular. I had reason to believe something bad had happened to Terry. Time to file an official report. I could keep Blaine's name out of it.

I headed straight to the police station in Wheaton. I was tempted to just handle it with a phone call, but I felt like I needed to look someone in the eye while filing my report. This was more than just an everyday misdemeanor and I had to know whether the police took my concerns seriously.

At the police station, I entered through a lobby and found a skinny little guy in street clothes behind a desk, on the phone. He finally hung up and greeted me with a terse, "Yes?"

"I'd like to report a missing person."

The phone rang and Mr. Bones jerked a thumb toward a wall bench. "Wait there. An officer will take your report." He snatched up the receiver. "Montgomery County Police, District Four, Rolland," he told the caller.

I meandered over to the bench, sat down, and checked my email by phone. But I kept an eye on the multitasking greeter, to make sure he told someone I was there.

My head still pounded and I did my usual seated mambo to keep the lower backache at bay. I stowed the phone and shut my eyes, in a lame attempt to ease the pain.

After what seemed like only a few minutes, I opened my eyes and checked the time. I'd been there an hour. Startled onto my feet, I went to check with Boney Rolland.

I walked over to the desk and planted my hands on the edge. "Remember me?"

Rolland squinted my way. "Missing person?"

"Right," The word came out bit louder than intended. "You said an officer would come take my report. I've been here over an hour."

"Well, I've been here since 6:30 A.M. So I've got you beat."

"Any idea how long it will be?"

"As soon as possible," he said. "After they've attended to the usual murders, rapes, and burglaries."

My headache suddenly worsened. I closed my eyes and leaned against the desk.

"Are you alright?" The man's voice seemed to come from a great distance.

When I didn't answer, I felt a touch on my arm. "Why don't you go home and call the report in?" Rolland said. "We'll send an officer to your house."

I opened my eyes and, straining to stay calm, I said, "Thanks. I'll do that." *Why didn't you tell me that in the first place?*

CHAPTER TWENTY-FOUR

Since I was no longer working for Blaine, I spent most of the day catching up on computer research I owed another client and took occasional breaks to do yoga stretches. Stretching my back provided a small measure of relief. The research gig was small change compared with what I could've earned from Blaine, but it would pay one or two bills.

An officer named Hillerman came by—eventually—to take my report. The man was a few inches taller than me with close-cropped brown hair, well-proportioned features, and an officious manner. He also looked just old enough to get a driver's license.

As I recounted events leading up to Terry's disappearance, I was very careful not to mention Blaine, his dead partner, or his missing daughter. I did throw in the fact that someone had tried to shoot me. For all the good that would do. As for Gorilla Man, I was the one who had tossed him to the ground. Discretion being the better part of common sense, I decided not to mention it.

Hillerman scratched his nose with the blunt end of his pen. "Let me get this straight. Someone took a shot at you, but you're reporting a missing person? Do you have any reason to think those things are connected?"

I racked my brain, but couldn't dredge up a thing that wouldn't involve Blaine in some manner. "Not really" was my sole response.

Hillerman eyed me in a way that suggested he didn't quite believe that. "You do realize that the shooting may have nothing to do with your friend? And that your friend may have chosen to disappear?"

"But why would he leave his cell phone behind?" And even as my words tumbled out, I knew how Hillerman would respond.

"A cell phone can be tracked. Maybe your friend doesn't want to be contacted or tracked. No offense, ma'am."

Ma'am? Jesus. "None taken," I said, clamping my lips shut on the profanities that were too close to the surface.

Hillerman was good enough to make out a separate report of the shooting. And after assuring him multiple times that I hadn't gotten a look at the shooter or otherwise had any clue as to who he was or why he would target me, Hillerman assured me that my report would get "all due attention," which I took to mean none. Unless, of course, the gunman who set his sights on me went on a genuine shooting spree—which I doubted would happen.

After the officer left, I took a moment to grab a cup of coffee and refocus my thoughts and then returned to my computer to get in some solid work. The phone rang. The caller ID indicated a blocked number. I sighed. *Answer or ignore?* I reached over and picked up.

"Is this Erica Jensen?" The caller was a male with a low and husky voice.

"Who's calling please?"

"Is this Erica Jensen?" The voice intensified and became angry.

"Nope. This is Queen Elizabeth. Who's calling please?"

"Stay away from the police, Jensen," the voice intoned. "And no more trips to Baltimore. Got that?"

I had no immediate response. The silence stretched into a small eternity. "Who the hell is this?"

"Never mind." The response was immediate. "Just do as I say or your friend will be in a world of shit."

CHAPTER TWENTY-FIVE

By now, the pounding in my skull had graduated to stabbing pain. "Which friend?" I asked, though I knew the answer.

But I was talking to dead air. I clicked disconnect and threw the phone down on the sofa.

Like a zombie, I stumbled toward the bathroom, where I kept an emergency stash of Oxy buried deep behind the toilet paper, shampoo, conditioner, and other toiletries stored under the sink. I grasped the pill bottle and almost ripped the top off in my haste to ease the unceasing pain.

Something stopped me from swallowing multiple tablets in one gulp. I'd been clean for so long. If I fell off the wagon now, where would it lead? If I OD-ed, what would happen to Terry? Then again, whoever had threatened me would be rid of me at that point. The horrid notion that Terry and I were better off dead passed through my mind.

I shook my head, like a dog shaking off water. *Buck up, Marine.* If my time in the armed services had been good for anything, it taught me that I had to stay strong, show no weakness, and quash any hint of self-pity.

I screwed the cap back on as if I was on autopilot. My thoughts turned to Nick, and I considered calling him for a pep talk. But I was plagued with worries about Terry and suspected there was little Nick could do to help with that.

After snapping out of my daze, I stowed the Oxy back under the sink, hoisted myself upright, and took two Tylenol.

Then I went for a walk around the block. Then another. By the end of the third go-round, I'd decided what to do.

I had no choice but to return to Baltimore and find out what Weis was doing with those artifacts—fake or otherwise. I had a sinking feeling that Terry's disappearance and the shooting were connected with them.

Before I left, I retrieved the slim file of information I'd managed to gather before Stuart Blaine dismissed me from his case. Again, I checked the diagram for any clues that I had missed earlier. Nothing stood up and waved at me.

When I got in the car, I checked the time. It was 1643 hours (4:43 P.M., in civvy-speak). Late in the day on a Friday. God knew what Weis would do, or where and with whom he'd do it. Melissa had been missing for a week or three, depending on whom you believed. And I'd been hired and fired in the span of five days. The situation was ridiculous. But I had to do something to help Terry. There had to be a connection between his disappearance and Blaine's case. Since it was my fault that he was in trouble, I needed to set things right.

φφφ

I drove up I-95 to Baltimore and found my favorite "Brian Weis surveillance spot" unoccupied. After easing my car into the space, I noticed Weis' SUV parked in the same place as before. I gazed at the vehicle, willing myself not to force my way into Weis' residence and beat the information out of him. That man was into something that smelled to high heaven. So who cared if I went a bit *Dirty Harry* on him? What would he do, call the cops?

I was fast reaching the point of not giving a damn what I did or to whom. I had been fired by a client I didn't trust, I had been used for target practice, and my friend was missing, maybe kidnapped or killed by Russian mobsters. The more I thought about all of this, the more my rage kicked in.

Rather than sit there with my thumb up my ass, I decided to go straight for Weis and damn the consequences. I got out of the car, slammed the door, and marched straight toward Weis' front door. After I pressed the bell, I waited, then pounded my fist on the door three times for good measure. To my surprise, Weis opened up. He leaned against the doorway, crossed his arms, and smirked at me.

"Last time we met," he said. "You ran away. Now you're back?"

"That's right, Brian," I spat. I held up my phone with the artifacts photo displayed. "Care to explain what these are?"

"I don't, actually." While I pocketed my phone, Weis began to close the door. I threw my weight full force against the door and it flew open so fast, it knocked Brian over backwards. He collapsed to the floor and smacked his head against it.

As he lay there in a daze, I walked inside and stood over him. My lower spine yapped at me once. I ignored it and powered on through . . . such is life with back injuries. I refuse to sit in a corner and sulk over them.

When Weis tried to move, I slammed him back down and pinned him by the shoulders. I straddled Weis' legs and moved one forearm across his throat. At that point, he lay very still.

"Now, if you're finished with the fun and games," I said. "Let's talk about those photos."

I could sense Weis' arm muscles tighten, as if to make a move. I drew back and slapped him hard, grabbed both his arms, and tucked his hands under my knees. Then I put my hands back on his shoulders.

My face hovered inches from his, as I barked like a drill sergeant. "Would you like me to snap your neck? That what you want, you little shit?"

I had no intention of murdering that worm, but he didn't need to know that.

Weis opened his mouth, licked his lips, but said nothing. I leaned over him and gripped his throat. He shook his head. "No," he croaked.

"Then what's the story with that stuff in the back of your SUV?"

"I'm just a courier," he said.

"What the hell does that mean? A courier for who?"

He shook his head again. I tightened my grip.

"Please." He blurted the word. "I don't want her to get into trouble."

"Who? Who are you protecting?"

"He's talking about me." A woman's soft voice piped up from within the house. I looked up and saw a backlit figure approach. From what I could see, her hair appeared to be brown, streaked with blonde, but I couldn't make out her facial features.

Could it be? Keeping a tight hold on Weis, I asked, "Are you Melissa Blaine?"

She shook her head. "My name is Jen Gardiner."

CHAPTER TWENTY-SIX

For a moment, I had no idea what to say. Jen approached me as one might a wounded animal.

"So what's your story?" I asked, once I'd found my tongue.

As she drew near, I was able to make out her expression, a mixture of bafflement and guilt.

"Who are you?" she asked. A fair question.

"I was hired to find a man who stole money," I said. "And while I was looking, I ran across a dead body and someone tried to kill me."

"I don't know anything about that," Jen said. Her gaze darted toward Weis and snapped back to me.

I stood up and backed away from Weis. He scuttled back and kept an eye on me, as he rose to his feet.

"How about we sit down and have a chat?" I said.

Jen nodded and looked at Weis, who shrugged. Jen led the way toward a small kitchen, with Weis behind her and me in the rear.

"Coffee?" Jen asked. I nodded. She grabbed a half-filled carafe off the burner and poured three mugs. Once we'd gotten our fixings (Jen offered milk, sugar, soy milk, fancy flavors—all that crap), we took our places around the vintage Formica dinette. We made a cozy threesome.

After a moment of quiet, I decided to get the conversational ball rolling. "Let me get this straight. Are the pictures on my phone of fake artifacts?"

Jen began to answer but hesitated. Weis touched her arm, in a wordless show of support. I sipped my coffee, thinking my hosts seemed about as dangerous as field mice.

I sighed. "Can you at least tell me who paid you to make the artifacts? I'm assuming they're fake?"

Jen finally nodded. "Yes, they are," she blurted. "Slava Kandinsky paid me to make them."

I turned toward Weis. "So that would put you in charge of transportation." His head bobbed forward once.

"Funny you should mention Kandinsky," I said. "It was his body I found."

Their faces turned such a ghastly pale, either they hadn't heard that he had been killed or they should both be awarded Oscars.

"Any idea who might've killed him?"

They shook their heads, looking numb.

"Okay," I said. "Those were the easy questions. Let's get down to brass tacks. Why were you"—I jabbed a finger toward Weis—"following me?"

Weis swallowed so hard, his neck seemed to spasm. "Our contact asked me to do that. He got worried after you started asking people around the art school about Melissa."

Like this should surprise me.

I pressed forward. "Did your contact tell you to cut my car's brake fluid lines?"

His gaze met mine, confused. "No."

"How did you know where to find me?"

"Our contact . . . " His voice trailed off. "He gave me the address of an auto repair shop and told me to look for a blue Fiesta."

Weis looked sincere and seemed unlikely to lie about this. *So, who the hell damaged my car?*

"Who is your contact?"

Weis shook his head. "He calls himself Mr. D." He must have sensed my discontent with that answer, because he added with haste, "That's all I know about him. The rest of the time I dealt with Mr. Kandinsky."

"What does Melissa have to do with this?"

Weis propped his head in his hands and rubbed his face, elbows on the table. "She introduced us to Mr. Kandinsky. Oh, shit."

I absorbed the response. If Kandinsky had stolen money, this could be where he'd spent it. "So, Slava Kandinsky paid you to make fake artifacts for his contacts? Is that how it works?"

Weis said, "Yep," so abruptly, it sounded like a grunt.

"Who are these contacts? Buyers? Wholesalers? What?"

"I don't know," he snapped. "We just get paid and do our job."

And whoever got the product probably figured out the scam, and Kandinsky had paid with his life. That was my guess. Oh, shit, indeed.

CHAPTER TWENTY-SEVEN

Digging for information bit by bit from these two was wearing me out, so I asked the $25,000 question: "Where is Melissa Blaine?"

Weis and Jen both gave me a hopeless look. "I don't know," Jen said.

"I thought you guys were friends," I said.

Jen heaved a sigh. "Yeah. Me, too."

"Did she even give a hint that she was leaving?"

Jen shook her head. Weis appeared on the verge of collapse.

"My own friend has apparently been kidnapped by your business associates," I said. "I hope, for your sake, that neither he nor Melissa have joined Kandinsky in the hereafter."

Weis peered at me. "Why would they kidnap your friend?"

"I was hoping you'd help me figure that out."

Weis frowned. "No clue." He hid his face with his hands again.

I forced a smile. "Well, we can't always get what we want."

φφφ

By the time I left the house, it was dark. I strode to the car, only to find a ticket for illegal parking tucked under the right windshield wiper. Great. Charm City was not living up to its nickname right now. I snatched the thing off the windshield and tossed it into the car.

After sliding behind the wheel, I grabbed the file and fished out my notes. By the light of my cell phone, I eyed my makeshift diagram of the major players in this fiasco. Possible connections were coming into focus now, but I didn't want to jump to any conclusions. There was also the matter of finding Terry.

I put the file back together and set it on the passenger seat. As I started the car, a vehicle pulled up and blocked the alley's closest exit. A dark limo. I threw my car into reverse and backed as fast as I dared.

My hands shook as my car swerved backwards down the alley. It was all I could do to keep from sideswiping a building in the dim light. I dared a swift glance at the limo. It hadn't moved. In the gloom, I could make out what seemed to be an intersecting alley. I careened backwards around the corner, saw a brick wall behind me, and paused to consider my next move. Nosing forward far enough to look both directions, I detected no movement from the limo on my left. On the right, the exit was partially blocked by a dumpster on one side and a car on the other.

Part of me fumed about getting a ticket for parking in an alley while these idiots blocked it at each end ticket-free, but I didn't have time to dwell on that. The more important question was, could I make it through the tiny exit?

Having little choice, I turned right and prayed that I could squeeze through.

I sped to the opening, then slowed to a crawl. It was a tight fit and then some. I yanked my left-side rearview mirror in to keep it from scraping the dumpster. Moving inch by inch, my car was almost halfway home, when another car appeared at the curb ahead of me.

The passenger door opened. A man emerged and approached my car, making hand motions, as if to guide me through. Yet, I felt little relief getting help from this apparent Good Samaritan. Not with that limo parked behind me.

As I moved forward, I tried to make out the license plate as it angled into view. It was barely legible under the nearby streetlamp. My peripheral vision spied more doors opening on my so-called savior's car. That was my cue. I gunned the engine and swerved onto the street, sending a small group of pedestrians scattering and eliciting a honk from another driver, but leaving my anonymous helpers in the dust.

CHAPTER TWENTY-EIGHT

As I barreled down the street, I took a quick glance in the rearview mirror. The men who came to my aid had disappeared, except for the silhouette of a leg slipping behind the car's open door. The car started to move toward me, the door shutting while the car was in motion. It was obviously much more powerful than mine—a full-size Ford or Chevy. If this had been a race, my Fiesta would be the tortoise to their hare.

I pressed the gas pedal as hard as I dared, looking both ways and praying as I blew through a stop sign. With a wrench of the wheel, I careered to the right down a side street. I swear my side of the car lifted off the ground. At least, it felt that way. When I checked the rearview mirror again, a car that could've been the one in pursuit rounded the turn I'd taken. I swung left onto another street, punched the gas, then turned left again.

By this time, I was buried deep within residential Baltimore City. Not a bad neighborhood, but one from which I had no clue about how to reach the interstate. I was startled into swerving to the opposite lane after spying a plastic garbage bag on the side of the road—a sight that sets the letters "IED" flashing through my brain. I eased on the brake and slowed enough to stop for the few seconds it took me to back the Fiesta into a tiny gap between two cars.

I had chosen the spot hoping that I'd go unnoticed if the car went by. It was between streetlights, creating a shadowy hideout between pools of light. Of course, if they did notice me, I was screwed. All they'd have to do is pull up alongside me and I'd be trapped. *Well done, Erica!*

Having few options, I shrugged it off and dove into my shoulder bag for a pen and paper, so I could scribble the car's license plate number before I forgot it. The act of writing it relieved me of the need to repeat it mentally—over and over— like the world's most annoying mantra.

I heard the car before I saw it and slid down below the steering wheel. The headlights glared above me, then dimmed slightly. From the sound of the motor, the vehicle seemed to be moving as fast as a snail. *Keep going!* I wanted to shout.

To my surprise, the car did just that. Even so, I waited ten minutes before extricating myself from my crouched position.

A quick scan revealed a street sign tinted orange in the glow of a sodium lamp. I reached for my cell phone and checked Google Maps. Adjusting the size with fumbling fingers disclosed the art school's location and reoriented me to mine. Now, to figure out how to reach the interstate without encountering those Good Samaritans.

CHAPTER TWENTY-NINE

I started the car and eased out onto the street. With no one in sight, I started to relax a little. My gaze swept back and forth as I moved through the darkness toward the main road. With no sign of my pursuers, I left the neighborhood feeling more secure by the second. The main road—four lanes that led to I-83—buzzed with commuters and whoever else might want to brave city roads at rush hour. Constant surveillance showed no sign of black limos or Good Samaritans. I made a beeline to the interstate and got the hell out of Dodge City, so to speak.

After an uneventful drive home, I pulled my car into the garage and left it in the space closest to the entrance. I trudged inside and climbed the two flights to my unit. While approaching my door, I spied a large plain white envelope tucked underneath it. *What now?*

I opened my door and toed the envelope inside. Unaddressed, but no doubt meant for me. It could contain a letter or anthrax. I shut the door and locked up tight, then retrieved a pair of latex gloves from the kitchen and pulled them on before opening my surprise delivery. Inside was one photo.

The man depicted looked like Terry, although it was hard to tell for sure. The lack of lighting and angle of the shot made it hard to determine the man's identity. He also looked like he'd had the living crap beaten out of him.

I recoiled at the sight but managed to recover rather quickly. My revulsion was dwarfed by rising anger and disgust. *What is this supposed to accomplish?* I could only hope that the victim wasn't Terry. *Shoot me, if you must, but leave my friends out of it.*

Too tired to think any further, I tossed the photo onto my coffee table. *Get a magnifying glass and examine the picture,* my conscience yelled. *Later!* I mentally shouted back. My lower back threw occasional sparks down my legs and up my spine. Frustration made my head pound again. It was all I could do not to scream.

Exhausted and in pain, I collapsed into bed fully clothed, but my brain was churning like crazy. So, I struggled to my feet and turned on the TV. Unfortunately, I'd left it on a news channel, which did nothing to improve my mood. Rather than channel surf, I snapped the damn thing off, made myself a pot of coffee (believe it or not, coffee for me, is both stimulating and relaxing), and tried to calm down by reading a book.

It was nearly half-past midnight when I finally felt ready for bed. I had just slipped under the covers when my cell phone rang. Answer or ignore? If it was the thugs who had sent that photo, the latter might be wiser. But, then again. My brain seemed to spasm. Then it cried, *you need sleep*!

The ringing stopped, then started again. I reached over and turned off the phone. A few minutes ticked by. Then, my land line jangled. I roused myself enough to reach the receiver, pick it up, and slam it down. Then, I turned off the ringer. So much for that.

It took a while for sleep to come. When it did, the dreams it brought were too much like being awake to be restful. I was plagued with a bizarre kaleidoscope of imagery. Being chased through a desert by Russians firing Kalashnikov rifles at me. Sidestepping a discarded soda can, which exploded in a cloud of fragments. A child's blood-streaked face emerging from the cloud, begging me not to shoot him. Bumping down a barely discernible road in a jeep with an aspiring pig farmer who'd end up dead right beside me.

I woke up sweating after hearing a loud bang. I stared at the ceiling in disbelief, but the banging continued. No explosions. Someone was knocking on my door.

CHAPTER THIRTY

At first, I thought I'd been hearing things. I lay there blinking, trying to get my bearings. The knocking resumed, even louder.

The watery light of dawn oozed in around the outline of the window shade. My bedside clock read 0730.

Oddly, my first thought was to call the police. My second was to grab the nearest blunt object and greet my visitor with it.

Ignore it, I thought. But my curiosity wouldn't let me. With everything that had happened, I should at least look through the peephole.

Even though the knocking had let up, I rolled out of bed, finger-combed my hair back, and crept to the door. I peered out and saw . . . no one.

Now awake and thinking, I ran to the window that overlooked the street in front of the building. There were no obvious signs of any of vehicles that had pestered me lately. Which is not to say they hadn't been there. Or weren't parked elsewhere.

Just in case, I retrieved a small pair of binoculars from my closet and my little notebook from my shoulder bag. Flipping to the page where I'd scribbled the license plate number, I returned to the window and scanned the lines of cars parked along both sides of the road. Neither the vehicles nor the plates I managed to make out were of interest.

This reminded me that I needed to look up the license plate. I'd get to that after a shower and some coffee. I let the shower pour over me for a good long while. I wanted to wash the memory of the last few days down the drain.

After finishing with my morning ablutions and throwing on a pair of jeans and a T-shirt that didn't smell, I made some coffee and did a few back stretches while waiting for the coffee to brew. After pouring a cup, I booted up my computer and signed into the database I needed.

I typed in the plate number. What came up was a keen disappointment. There was no record of the number.

"What do you mean?" I asked the computer, as if it could hear me.

I tried again. No better luck the second time.

This could only mean that I'd written down the wrong number.

I pounded my fist on the desk. "Damn it!"

Attempting fast getaways and noticing plate numbers just don't go together.

CHAPTER THIRTY-ONE

I was tired of thinking, tired of dealing with the fallout from a case I was no longer hired to handle. It wore me out just sitting in front of my computer. With my eyes closed, my thoughts began to drift.

What I really needed to do was relax. One thing I'd learned since returning home from the war was that I needed to tune out every now and then. Taking a meditation class had helped a little bit with that, but unfortunately, I didn't use what I had learned as often as I should. But every once in a while, I'd give it a try . . . and this seemed like the perfect time.

I closed my eyes and sat upright—not ramrod straight, as if at attention, but comfortably upright, as if my head were a balloon attached to a string. I tried to be aware of any tension, noting each body part and relaxing it. Face, eyelids, jaw, neck, shoulders, arms, hands, then downward.

After fully relaxing, I took a few deep breaths, mentally unfocused and, with the aid of a mantra, let go of conscious thoughts, or tried to. Even now, it seems a bit unnatural for me to focus on not focusing. I decided to chalk that up to my lack of regular practice.

Thing was, each attempt at meditation seemed to make the next try easier. This should've encouraged me to treat it as I would treat brushing my teeth—make it a habit. But some impatient inner demon insisted on spending time doing other things. And what little patience I had started with was wrung out of me by the time my last tour in Afghanistan ended. I thought about this and then tried not to think—to let those thoughts go and allow the mantra to take over.

Time passed. Maybe 15 minutes. That was about as much non-thought as my mind could handle. When I reopened my eyes, the world seemed like a better place. I was ready to return to the problems at hand—and maybe even solve them. Without any effort, one notion for a solution clicked into place.

Maybe I hadn't gotten the license plate entirely wrong. Perhaps I was off by a letter or number. I could go through countless iterations, but it might be wise to try a few of the obvious ones.

I checked the plate number. There was one letter that could have been a "C" or a "G." I thought it was the former, so I tried running the plate number again with the substitution. No luck.

The numbers weren't ambiguous. A "7" wouldn't be confused for a "4", for instance. I focused on the letters instead. Maybe the "O" was actually a "Q". I tried again. Nothing.

The third letter was one I doubted would be confused for another. I figured I'd try substituting both of the other two and see where it got me.

To my surprise, I got a hit. However, a look at the details revealed the car to be a Porsche owned by a 63-year-old woman who lived in a toney section of Baltimore.

In other words, I may have hit the lucky number, but the plate was probably stolen.

I figured, "Okay. It's not the end of the world." Knowing that the license plate may have been stolen was informative too.

I didn't figure the Russian mob operated this way. It was much more likely that my unwanted companions were the kind of lowlifes who might have screwed around with Terry.

That reminded me about the photo. I got up and retrieved it from the coffee table. The man pictured resembled Terry, but was it him? And what about the apparent bruises and blood? A closer look was in order.

From a junk drawer in my kitchen, I dug out a magnifying glass. An old-fashioned, round magnifying glass, stuck on the end of a short, black handle. Standard issue private eye gear for Sherlocks of any era.

I studied the photo through the magnifier and looked for obvious signs of retouching and Photoshopped effects. While I can't claim expertise in spotting faked photos, there was something a bit off about the look of this one. The bruises were a bit too monochromatic. The skin around them too smooth.

Or maybe that was just false hope talking to me.

I was still scrutinizing the picture when I heard knocking at my door again. I placed the photo and magnifier down as gently as possible, padded toward the door, and peered through the peephole. A man I didn't recognize stood on the other side. He wore a dark suit, tie, and white shirt. He didn't carry a clipboard, so he wasn't here to sell magazines or proselytize for any religion. Apparently.

After a moment, he knocked again. I moved toward my bedroom and called, "Hang on."

Not wanting to keep my visitor waiting, I ducked into the bedroom and found my Sig P320 handgun. I keep a gun for emergencies only. It seemed like my life was becoming one long emergency. I tucked the gun into the back of my waistband, hoping I wouldn't need to use it.

CHAPTER THIRTY-TWO

After one last peek at the man outside my apartment, I made sure the chain was in place and opened up. Frankly, the chain was a joke and could easily be kicked in. Thus, the need for my gun.

"Erica Jensen?" The stranger asked. He appeared benign, but you can't be sure of such things.

"Who are you?"

"Agent Phipps, FBI." He reached inside his jacket.

"Careful," I said. "Move your hands slowly." I pulled out the gun, letting it hang at my side.

Agent Phipps held a hand palm forward, placating. "I'm just getting my ID."

"Right. You should have had *that* out before you knocked." I started to close the door on him.

Phipps pushed back. "We need to talk."

"On a Saturday?"

"I'm sorry to ruin your weekend," he said. "But FBI agents are like the Pinkertons. We never sleep."

"What's there to talk about?"

"Slava Kandinsky."

Kandinsky? This could be about his mob connections or the forged artifacts.

Curiosity got the best of me. "Let's see that ID then."

After the man calling himself Phipps showed me what looked like a proper FBI badge, I asked for a business card. He handed one to me. "Hang on," I said, shutting the door in his face. I replaced the gun in my waistband and ran to my computer.

After a quick check online, I verified the number on the card as that of the local FBI office. A quick call to the number connected me with a voice mail greeting system that left little doubt that my visitor was an actual agent.

Only then did I unlock the chain and usher him into the living room, waving an invitation to sit on the sofa. I kept an eye on him as I sat on the opposite end, not bothering to offer a drink.

"I assume you know who Slava Kandinsky is?" he said.

My stomach clenched. "What makes you say that?"

"You've been investigating his associates." It wasn't a question.

"What do you need with me?" I asked, ignoring his non-question.

Phipps assumed an expression so serious his face seemed to turn to stone. "These are dangerous men you've become involved with. The best course of action would be for you to back off and leave this to the professionals."

"Any progress in finding out who took a shot at me?" I struggled not to shout the words.

Phipps blinked. "Who are you working for?"

I shook my head. "Don't you love when someone answers a question with another question?"

"I'm serious."

"So am I. And I don't have a client. I'm just trying to stay alive and figure out what happened to a friend."

Phipps rose suddenly and took a step toward me. "Listen," he started.

He didn't get far. The minute he rose, so did a memory from Afghanistan. The flashback came on suddenly as the blackout had occurred with Gorilla Man at Terry's place. My current stress level was clearly eating at me. An image of a shadow that loomed during a residence check in Kandahar played like a movie. I moved back a step and chopped Phipps' temple with the side of my hand. This stunned the man enough to let me kick out and slam my foot into his groin. He doubled over, gasping, and collapsed to the floor, grazing the coffee table as he did, snapping me from the past to my present condition, back injury and all. I'd pay for that later.

On instinct, I pulled the gun and trained it on him. "Don't move."

Phipps looked up at me and again raised a hand. "I'm sorry. They warned me about this. But attacking a federal agent isn't your best choice here. But I'm aware that you served in the military. I hope that'll give you more incentive to cooperate."

Heat radiated up my face, as shame and embarrassment overwhelmed me.

"Have we done this before?" I asked.

Phipps shook his head. "Not us, but another agent looking for a fellow named Terry Morris."

Another agent? I remembered Gorilla Man. *Sorry, dude.*

But Two-Bit Terry? "What's your interest in him?"

"Following a lead," he non-answered the question. "I'm more interested in Kandinsky."

"And what's so interesting about him?"

"He's been linked with terrorists."

I went from squinting to frowning. "Are you saying that Slava Kandinsky was a terrorist?"

"Not exactly. He wasn't a terrorist, but he was dealing with them."

"So he was supporting terrorists?"

Phipps shook his head. "Worse than that. He was ripping them off."

CHAPTER THIRTY-THREE

I took a moment to absorb what he'd just said. If it were true, it could explain a few things.

"Mind if I get up?" Agent Phipps asked in a mildly aggrieved tone of voice.

Pulled back to reality, I tucked the gun back into my waistband and helped him to his feet.

"Have a seat." I tried to reassure the agent with an amiable tone. Or at least a reasonable facsimile of one. "Would you like a drink?"

"This won't take long," he assured me. The words "assuming you let me talk" remained unspoken.

After we'd re-settled onto the sofa, Phipps continued. "Slava Kandinsky deals in smuggled artifacts for the Russian mafia. Antiquities trafficking turns profits in the billions every year. Terrorists have been tapping this market for a very long time—long before the 9/11 attacks. In fact, looted artifacts are a major funding source for fundamentalist terrorist groups."

By now, my head was spinning with possibilities. "What was Kandinsky's role in this business?"

"We think Kandinsky served as middleman between traffickers and interested resellers. You wouldn't believe his client list. We're talking everything from major auction houses and museums to ISIS and Hezbollah."

I put two and two together. "Kandinsky was skimming from the profits made from resellers?"

Phipps nodded.

"So how can I help you?" I asked.

"You can start by telling me who you work for. Why are you investigating Kandinsky?"

I gave it a moment's thought. What did I owe Blaine? The man had tossed me aside like a used tissue. Even so, I hesitated to simply tell all. Particularly since Blaine suspected Kandinsky of stealing from him.

"My client thought Kandinsky was embezzling from his company," I offered. "He has since let me go."

Phipps peered at me, as if trying to x-ray my mind. Typical cop look.

"Why did your client fire you?" he asked.

I shrugged. "Guess he felt like he wasn't getting his money's worth."

"Could it have been that you were getting too close to something he didn't want you to find out?" Phipps said.

"I doubt it," I replied, in all honesty.

Phipps nodded, but his gaze bore into me. "I suggest you tell me the name of your client, just in case. If you're not completely sure he wasn't involved, it would be in your best interest."

I had to admit the man might have a point. Especially since Blaine had been vehement about keeping the cops out the picture.

"All right. It was his partner, Stuart Blaine."

"Hmm." Phipps retrieved a small spiral pad and pen from his breast pocket and jotted notes. "Anything else you can tell me about Kandinsky that might help?"

"You *will* keep my name out of this?" This was getting nerve-racking.

"Of course, to the extent that's possible." His qualifier made me less than fully confident.

"Talk to Brian Weis." I spelled the last name for him. "He lives in Baltimore near MICA—the art school in Baltimore. He and a woman named Jen Gardiner were doing business with Kandinsky."

Phipps scribbled some more. "Anything else?"

"That's all that comes to mind."

Phipps rose and tucked the notebook and pen away. Apparently, our interview was over.

"Hang on," I said before Phipps could leave. "There's someone out there gunning for me. Is that person connected with Kandinsky, the Russians, the terrorists, or what?"

"I'm sorry, but I can't help you there."

"Do you mean that you don't know or you won't tell me?" I asked through gritted teeth.

His look of shock seemed real enough. "Of course I would tell you, if I knew. This is the first I've heard of anyone making an attempt on your life."

I sighed inwardly. The sniper had taken his or her shot only yesterday. It seemed like a month ago. Only time would tell if another version of the Serial Sniper had returned to the DC area.

"I take it from your questions that you haven't recovered the money Kandinsky allegedly embezzled?" I added.

"Not yet." Spoken as if it were practically a done deal.

I nodded. "Okay, thanks."

We walked to the door together. "If you think of anything else, you have my card," Phipps said before leaving.

CHAPTER THIRTY-FOUR

I returned to my computer and scanned news headlines. Nothing in there about sniper shootings, including the one aimed at me. I pondered this. *Why would someone take a shot at me? Who'd be threatened by me?*

The case file sat on the coffee table. I grabbed it and moved into my small kitchen. Rocky waited outside on the windowsill. I set the file on my tiny kitchen table so I could retrieve the peanut jar from its shelf and fish out his breakfast.

"Hey, Rocky." I slid the window and screen open, then addressed him in my most squirrel-friendly tone. "Want a peanut?"

Rocky focused on the hand-delivered nut. My rodent friend grabbed it from my fingers and stuffed it in his mouth. A liberal sprinkling of nuts met the same fate, and Rocky's cheeks were soon bulging.

"Nice to know we can count on at least one thing, eh, kiddo?"

Rocky gave me a quizzical look, like "What?" Ah, to be non-sentient.

I fixed myself a quick breakfast of toasted English muffin with butter and Marmite. As I polished it off, I reviewed the chart I had made while working on Blaine's case. A vague suspicion arose in the back of my mind . . . something that might help me connect the dots on my diagram.

I reviewed the names and drew a few more lines. This showed what I knew, but something was missing. Things I couldn't know for sure. Speculating on possibilities based on my knowledge was the next step.

Kandinsky, connected with the Russian mob and terrorists, may or may not have embezzled money from Blaine. The money was still missing. And Kandinsky had a son who refused to take part in something his father proposed.

Kandinsky used art students to create forgeries and was ripping off the Mob or terrorists or both, skimming profits from the sale of the items to museums and auction houses.

A vague suspicion was beginning to take shape, but there was a missing link in the chain of events. Kandinsky's son. According to his letter, he wasn't involved in his father's business. This got me thinking.

Even if Kandinsky's son hadn't been involved in ripping off terrorists or mobsters, that didn't mean he was completely out of the picture. But where did he fit, if he fit anywhere in the scheme?

CHAPTER THIRTY-FIVE

Before I could delve into the matter of Kandinsky's son, I had business to attend to.

I grabbed the Blaine file, stuffed the photo of Terry inside, and readied myself for an excursion.

By the time I hit the road, it was close to 1030 hours. I headed straight to Terry's apartment. I needed to give it one last look to make sure I hadn't missed a clue.

I lucked out on the weather. According to the forecast, at least three days of sunshine were in store. I cracked the windows to let the balmy early autumn breeze flow through the car. Technically, early September was still summer and it felt like it—sans the stifling humidity of a typical Maryland July or August.

The flow of air as I drove was like bath water, and its caress should've been relaxing, but it wasn't. My mind still churned with thoughts of where Terry was and what had happened to him.

Keenly alert, my gaze hopped like a flea on a griddle from the road before me to the rearview and sideview mirrors. As best as I could see, no one was following me. Being hounded by too many people made me doubly cautious, especially with the destination I had in mind.

After I arrived at Terry's place, I used my bump key to enter. There were no obvious changes. Other than the low murmur of the TV in the next apartment, the place was quiet. I started with the living room, checking for scraps of paper, address books, receipts, anything at all. As I searched, the TV upstairs was turned off and an eerie hush fell over the place. When I reached the kitchen, the refrigerator cycled on with a loud, metallic click. I jumped an inch, and my heart started to pound like crazy.

After a thorough search of the kitchen and bath, I moved to the bedroom. I peeked under the bed and did a double take. No sign of Terry's phone. Was this a good sign or a bad one?

I continued to scour the room for clues as to Terry's whereabouts. The exercise felt futile and repetitious. I stopped and sat on the edge of the bed. If insanity was doing the same thing over and over and expecting a different result, I was definitely insane.

I closed my eyes, and my mind drifted back to when Terry and I had met. It was on the boardwalk in Ocean City. A summer day, years before I enlisted, when life seemed to hold the promise of an existence better than my reality.

Images from those times floated through my head, like my flashbacks to Afghanistan, except they were pleasant. My eyes snapped open, and I smacked the heel of my hand against my forehead. *Could the answer be this simple?*

CHAPTER THIRTY-SIX

I hurried back to my apartment to grab a few essentials—night shirt, toothbrush, and toothpaste. If I had to stay overnight, the bare essentials would do.

After hastily stuffing these items into a backpack, I added a change of underwear. That was really all the clothes I would need.

I decided against throwing in the Sig. I had no permit to carry and was already on thin ice legally by simply doing a private investigator's job without a state-sanctioned license. Besides, where I was headed, I had no reason to think I was in danger.

I grabbed my luggage, such as it was, locked up my apartment, and hurried to the car. I headed south toward the Beltway, and made my way to Route 50. From there, it was a straight shot east to Ocean City.

φφφ

Traffic was relatively light. No doubt a few of my fellow travelers were taking advantage of the good weather and the relative lack of crowds at the beach resort during the off-season. You could go to Ocean City as late as October and still enjoy warm weather without the irritating crush of great hordes of tourists.

Endless fields rolled by and the pungent odor of manure tinged the fragrance of soybean fields, corn stalks, and summer wheat. Driving through air perfumed by fertilizer was a small price to pay for the warm late-summer breeze.

Easton, Cambridge, Salisbury … it seemed to take forever to get there. Even though it was only a two-hour drive.

I finally reached Berlin, and from there, it was only a short distance to the water and the Route 50 bridge into the resort town. I wanted to find a parking place near the Boardwalk, and mercifully, there were plenty to choose from, lots more than during the height of tourist season. I nabbed a good one and hustled up the walkway toward the bar where Terry used to share an upstairs apartment with one of the ride operators.

The place, which had been a popular dive before my time, was as seedy as I remembered it. Mismatched wooden tables and chairs were scattered around the horseshoe-shaped bar. I perched on the cracked upholstery of a teetering stool and waved to the barkeep. The man aimed his dark button-like eyes, surrounded by wrinkles from too much sun, my way and approached with the speed of a sedated sloth.

"Does Dell still live upstairs?" I asked.

"No one lives upstairs." He grabbed a rag and wiped an invisible spot on the counter.

I pasted on a smile. "Any idea where Dell lives now?"

"You buying a drink or what?"

"Sure," I said. "You got root beer?"

The bartender pulled a sour expression. "No."

"Any kind of cola then. Not too much ice."

The man shuffled off to fill my order. By the time he returned with my drink, I had laid a $20 bill on the counter in front of me.

"You can keep the change, if I find the service up to par." I smiled wider.

The bartender looked me over. "This your idea of a bribe?"

"No, but this is." I added another twenty and dangled a third over it.

He nodded, humming what sounded like an assent.

"Suppose you could dig up an address for Dell?" I asked.

The old man rubbed his chin. "I suppose."

CHAPTER THIRTY-SEVEN

Dell's place was located on a side street off the north end of Ocean Highway. Little more than a shack, the small building cowered behind a row of tall marsh grasses. In an apparent attempt to make the place look more like a California or Florida resort, the owner had planted a hapless palm tree in the yard. The plant thrust its way upward, but it was dying, its dry brown fronds drooping listlessly despite the breeze.

A small walkway poked through a gap in the overgrown grass. I plunged through and approached the door.

A few seconds after a quick knock, the door opened a crack. A rheumy eye peered out. "Yeah?"

"Hi, my name's Erica. Are you Dell?"

The eye squinted. "Whatever it is, I'm not buying."

"Good, because I'm not here to sell anything. I'm looking for Terry."

"What?" It came out like a bark. "What's your game, girlie? How did you get this address?"

I gave him my hardest look. "I'm an old friend of Terry's. You used to live with him, back in the day. Frankly, I'm worried about him." I held up the photo. "Can I assume that you are Dell? If you are, this should worry you, too."

The eye widened. It's gaze darted between me and the photo. "Hang on." The door closed.

Be patient, I told myself. Either he's here or Dell's going to call him.

I was counting the limp fronds on the doomed palm when the door opened wide. A man about my height and three times my age faced me. Slightly stooped with thinning gray hair, the man waved an invitation to enter.

"I'm Dell. Come on in," he said. "Sorry about the wait, but you can't be too careful these days."

The entrance led directly to the living room, furnished like the stereotypical man cave. A worn, stained sofa stretched against one wall opposite a flat-screen TV. A recliner and a coffee table strewn with magazines and remotes finished off the ensemble. On the right, I spied part of the kitchen, the rest of which hid behind a wall.

"Have a seat," Dell said. "Terry will be here in just a minute. He was asleep. Would you like some coffee?"

"Sure," I said, eyeing the sofa stains before I perched on the edge of a cushion. "With a little milk, if you have it." I usually take my coffee black. And fresh. But based on my first impression, I figured the coffee would not be top quality.

Terry emerged from a hallway on the left that no doubt led to the bedrooms. To my relief and amazement, he looked unharmed.

I leapt from the sofa and practically tripped over the coffee table running toward him. "I've been worried sick about you. Ever since I got this." I gave him the photo. "Even before that. Since I found your cell phone under your bed at home, dead."

Terry's eyes telegraphed regret. "I'm sorry I wasn't able to tell you, but those computer geeks I told you about. They were getting seriously annoying. I needed to hide out."

"Did you consider calling the police?"

He shook his head. "That wouldn't have been in anyone's interest. Get my drift?"

Loud and clear, I thought. "And you didn't take your phone, because you didn't want . . . "

"I didn't want them to track me."

I thought about that for a few seconds. "How the hell did it end up under your bed?"

Terry shrugged. "It was kind of my joke on them. I figured if they tried to track my phone it would simply lead to my place. And if they searched my place, all they'd find is my phone."

"Looks like the joke was on me," I said, snatching the photo back from him. "Would your angry geek clients know anything about this?" I added, waving the picture around.

He frowned. "Doubtful. More likely someone else took advantage of my absence to play head games with you."

CHAPTER THIRTY-EIGHT

My relief at seeing Terry alive gave way to annoyance. "I'm not your minder. But you might've at least let me know you had to go underground." I gave him a push, and he stumbled back.

"I would've if I'd had time," he countered.

I took a deep breath and nodded. The smell of fresh coffee infused the room. Dell tottered in with two steaming mugs in hand.

"Thank you," I said, accepting an offered mug. Surprise, surprise—the coffee did not disappoint.

A million questions raced around in my head. Were the people who followed me the same ones who were after Terry? Would they be the sort who would take a rifle shot at me?

"You just going to stand there or what?" Terry sounded amused.

"Just trying to figure a few things out," I said.

I returned to my perch on the couch and sipped my coffee. Definitely fresh. I could've skipped the milk.

Terry joined me on the sofa and waited for more of my story. Dell stretched out on the recliner.

"Would these geeks coming after you have reason to sic a sniper on me?"

"What?" Terry looked appalled.

"Yes, really," I said. "I guess it's open season on ex-Marine drug addicts."

"Not funny," he said.

"Couldn't agree more. So uh . . . why would your business associates want to kill me?"

His brow furrowed with concern, and he shook his head. "Can't imagine why."

"Are you sure it's the geeks who are after you?" I asked.

"Who else?" He waved a hand.

"What about the letter you translated for me? Anyone else know about that?"

"No way." Terry looked indignant.

No one but the University of Maryland professor, and I'd been followed to Maryland by Weis. Or at least someone connected to him.

I looked straight into Terry's eyes. "Do your clients have mob connections?"

"Honestly, I don't know. I don't ask those kinds of questions." He didn't look away from me.

Assuming the answer was yes, who were those guys in the car with the stolen license plate?

I sipped more coffee. It was damn good.

"I doubt the sniper was trying to kill me," I muttered.

"Just warn you off?" Terry asked. "From what? What do I have to do with it?"

"Maybe nothing."

Dell raised his mug. "More coffee?"

"Yes, thanks," I said. "Just black this time."

φφφ

It was late by the time I got back. Staying overnight in Ocean City had been an option, but I felt the need to get home and get to the bottom of whatever the hell was going on.

I studied my flowchart of names again. Then I tore a blank sheet off a writing pad and started scribbling fast as I could. The resulting brain dump was a disorganized mess of semi-decipherable words. But it jolted my brain into thinking outside the constraints of my flowchart.

I sensed an answer before one could fully form, but it was there. When the thought became coherent, it came at me like cold water thrown right in my face.

The answer had always been there. Perhaps I couldn't have imagined it. In any case, I hadn't wanted to see it.

CHAPTER THIRTY-NINE

I checked the time. It was 0030. A little late to be calling anyone, but I speed-dialed Nick, my new intrepid journalist mentor, with the hope that he'd be up. Much to my relief, he answered.

"Are you okay?" he asked. Not an unreasonable question given the hour.

"I'm fine," I said. "Have you ever written about smuggling or its connections to terrorism?"

"I never had a story run, but I have done some poking around."

"To the best of your knowledge, do these smugglers use computer hackers?" I asked.

This elicited a "hmmm" from the other end. "It's likely that they do, since so much crime involves computers these days. How exactly they might use them I couldn't say."

I considered the implications. Nick eventually said, "When I saw your caller ID, I was afraid you were having a crisis."

"What makes you think this isn't one?"

"The questions you're asking—I mean, I thought you were having a mental—" Nick faltered. "You know what I mean, right?"

I nodded, like the guy could see me. "I know. It's late, but I need help and wanted to run these ideas by you while they were still fresh in my mind."

"Erica?" Nick's voice had a razor-sharp edge. "What's going on?"

"I'm not sure, but I intend to find out."

φφφ

The next morning at approximately 0920, I drove back up to Baltimore to visit MICA again. I stopped in at Java Joe's first to check out one of my hunches. I didn't recognize the man behind the counter, but the woman seemed familiar. As I approached, the man moved to the register.

I ordered a medium cappuccino, and after paying the cashier, I approached the woman who would be making the drink.

"Remember me?" I asked.

She gave me a blank, I-see-a-lot-of-people look. After a moment, her eyes sparked with recognition.

"You were looking for Melissa," she said.

I nodded and checked her name tag. Elle.

"That's right, Elle," I said. "I assume you still haven't seen or heard from her."

She shook her head. "I wish I could help."

"How about this guy?" I held up my phone and displayed a photo I'd taken of Kandinsky and the young man I assumed was his son.

"Just a sec." The espresso machine roared as she fixed my cappuccino. She handed me the drink and stared at the image.

"The older one. That's the guy I told you about—Mr. Macchiato."

"How about the younger man?"

She looked at the photo again, this time more closely. "He does look familiar. May I?" She reached for the phone, and I handed it off.

Elle studied the picture. "I think I have seen him. Maybe. The guy I'm thinking of was a bit older than this."

"Could the man in this picture be the one you are thinking of when he was younger?"

She nodded and handed back my phone. "Definitely."

Now that was interesting. "Where have you seen him? Was he with Melissa by any chance?"

"I've seen him here and at the art school. Sometimes with Melissa."

Interesting. Make that very interesting. As I tucked my phone into my shoulder bag, Elle added, "I don't know if that's much help."

"More than you know," I said. Assuming my developing theories panned out.

CHAPTER FORTY

I speed-dialed Nick again to see what he had learned from his sources. According to his DOJ contacts, artifact smuggling was not only linked with the Mob, but was definitely being used to finance terrorist activities. All the federal intelligence agencies— CIA, NSA, Homeland Security (that big umbrella that seems to include everyone else)—were on this.

"Here's a hypothetical," I said. "Suppose someone involved in ripping off terrorists wanted to disappear. Any idea who could help them do that?"

"Other than witness protection?" Nick said. "There are actually people who do this for a living. Help other people stay under the radar, that is."

"I know that." A hint of annoyance crept into my voice. The words that came out of my mouth were sharper than intended, so I stopped for a few seconds and then continued in a more reasonable tone. "Do you know anyone in particular who does this?"

Nick gave me the name of a private eye in DC—Alex Kingsley. I had to give the woman props in the cool name department. Alex Kingsley, P.I. Could have been a new Netflix series. I gave her a call.

After introducing myself and explaining who had referred me, I told her I needed to find someone who I suspected was taking great pains to stay hidden. "I've done a bit of skip tracing and repo work, but I could use your advice as someone who helps people stay off the grid. Any tips at all on how to discover them."

"I tell them time and again not to stay in touch with anyone from their old life, but they do it anyway," she said. "The problem is people really don't want to leave their old lives. They're usually running away from something they'll never escape—themselves."

Figures.

φφφ

I decided to take a bit of a risk. I'm not on Facebook or Twitter, so my clients come to me by personal referral only. And I can't think of a soul I'd want to connect with through social media. But I took the plunge and opened a Facebook account under the slightly different name "Melinda Blaine", using the photo Melissa's father had provided as the profile picture. Then, I searched for her old friend Katie Saunders, verified her status as a teaching assistant at Columbia University, and sent her a friend request. I waited, but not for long.

My request went unaccepted, but within a day, I got a message back: WTF?

The response spawned numerous guesses. Time to nail down the truth.

φφφ

With advice from Alex Kingsley, I did a bit more poking around. Then I called Nick to thank him again for the referral. "Just so you know, I'm leaving town for a while."

"What's up? Where are you off to?" he asked.

"Better you don't know."

"Erica." Spoken like a warning. "What are you doing now?"

"It's about that case I had. There's unfinished business."

"Are you sure you don't need help?" Nick said.

I laughed. "I'm never sure of that. But I should probably manage this alone."

Nick grunted what might have been assent. "Okay, but don't forget. I'm willing to help."

"I won't forget," I said. "You're on my phone as my emergency contact. Please don't forget about me."

CHAPTER FORTY-ONE

I headed north on I-95 toward New York City, without a clue about where to spend the night. Traffic was the usual onslaught, but at least it wasn't a holiday. It took only four hours before the distinctive skyline of Gotham appeared in the distance.

The thought of driving into Manhattan gave me a headache, but I didn't want to leave my car. I made my way through the Lincoln Tunnel, plagued by thoughts of maneuvering through a sea of taxis and the cost of parking. Not to mention the $12.50 I paid to use the tunnel. But I was on a mission.

I had to confirm what I suspected was going on. In this case, I had to go directly to the source. Another phone call simply wasn't going to cut it. Besides, there were other matters to attend to. As long as I was in the area, I'd take care of them in person.

Before making this trip, I'd taken the precaution of looking up a few details online. I approached Columbia University's Morningside Heights campus, and there I had my pick of either on-street parking or one of several parking garages. Trying to decipher New York City's on-street parking signs wasn't worth the migraine, so I settled on a garage. I might not have a client to cover my costs, but getting to the bottom of things would be worth the expense.

From the garage, it was a pleasant walk to the campus. Autumn in New York is much nicer than its summers. Most of the trees were green, but some had leaves edged with gold and orange. The air was warm and gentle, without the previous months' intense heat and stickiness. And the campus provided an oasis of calm within the bustle of the city. I had written down the location of Katie Saunders' office, but I asked a passing student for directions, just to be sure.

I made my way through the building to Katie's office, hoping no one would stop me or ask for a student ID. No one did. Was that just dumb luck? Or can people just wander in off the street any time? When I knocked on Katie's door, a female voice invited me to come in.

I recognized her right away from her Facebook page—light brown hair, mid-twenties, hazel eyes, studious, pretty. She gave me the once over. "Are you in one of my classes?"

"No, Katie," I said. "I'm Erica Jensen."

The look on her face said, go away. Instead, I entered and closed the door behind me.

"You and I need to have a talk," I said. "About Melissa Blaine."

CHAPTER FORTY-TWO

Katie's gaze skittered about the office, as if looking for an escape hatch. I approached her desk and sat down, uninvited, in one of the guest chairs.

"Where is she?" I asked.

"I . . . I already told you. I don't know."

I leaned forward. "You're not a good liar. I think you do know. And you better start talking."

She threw me a scornful look. "Or what?"

"Or I call the cops."

Katie shifted in her desk chair. "I don't know . . . anything."

"You know enough." I rose, planted my hands on her desk, and leaned over it until my face was inches from Katie's. Yoga had done wonders for my battered back. "I've been threatened, shot at, and fired by a client who said he was looking for his daughter. That's enough to make me think there's something going on here. And, whatever it is, I think there's a reason my client wanted to keep the police out of it."

I thought about grabbing her by the shirtfront, but didn't. "You're going to tell me what you know about Melissa. Now."

φφφ

Back in Maryland, I went directly to the Blaine residence. I left my car on the street and hiked up the driveway toward the grand entrance. Three sharp raps on the door and it opened a crack. Blaine eyed me through the gap.

"What are you doing here?" he snapped.

"Where's Jeeves the Butler these days?" I asked. "He didn't answer the door the last time I was here either."

"None of your damn business," he said. "Now, unless you have a reason to see me, I suggest you leave."

"Or what?" I asked. "You'll call the cops?"

Blaine said nothing. That stumped him.

He tried to shut the door, but I slammed a hand against it and stiff-armed it open. It flew back and Blaine staggered away from me as I entered.

"You said you didn't want the police involved in your affairs," I continued. "Since we met, I've discovered why. You knew Kandinsky was skimming from the Russians. You knew, and you wanted your share."

Blaine's face contorted with rage. "You're guessing."

"Am I? You're forgetting something, Stu. I look for assets. That's what I do. If I had to, I could track down all the accounts you could create in the Caymans or any other tax-sheltered country you can name."

"Then, do it," he said. "See what you find."

"I don't have to," I said. "I've found Melissa."

The anger in his expression morphed into one of longing. Or hunger.

"Where is she? Is she all right?"

I reached into my shoulder bag and pulled out a folded sheet of paper. "Here's your answer," I said, handing it to him.

Blaine unfolded the paper and his eyes bugged out. "No!"

"Yes."

"No way." He shook his head. "No way is she dead."

"Feel free to check the records office in Broward County, Florida," I said. Then I turned to leave. "Case closed."

CHAPTER FORTY-THREE

My business with Blaine was finished, but I hadn't wrapped everything up just yet. After a dramatic exit from my former client's house, I went home, caught a few hours' sleep, and hit the road again. In an abundance of caution, I bought a burner phone and left my cell at home. I also used a map to find my way rather than rely on GPS.

The map included directions given to me (under only the slightest duress) by Katie. It led to a post office in Charlotte, North Carolina.

I backed my car into a space beside a sandwich shop far enough from the post office to go unnoticed, but close enough to watch the entrance. My first day of surveillance was a complete bore, as were my second and third. Now and then, I moved the car so I could walk to the shop and stake out the place while scarfing down a sandwich at a window table. For the most part, no one seemed to notice me. I slept in the car and stayed at my post while sneaking in a few minutes here and there for a hurried pit stop or to grab a quick bite to eat at the deli.

The fourth day finally bore fruit. The man entering the post office looked a good bit like the photo I had of Kandinsky's son. Less than a minute later, he reappeared and walked around to the back of the building. I started the car and crept toward the post office, pretending to look for a space.

A green pickup truck nosed out onto the street. My quarry was behind the wheel. He turned left, so I pulled into the drive that led to a parking lot, making as if to take his spot. After a quick three-point turn, I left the same way I'd come in and hastened to catch up with the pickup, making sure to keep two or three cars between us.

We took a fairly well-traveled, but hardly crowded, highway into the surrounding countryside. As we went deeper into the Great Smoky Mountains, traffic thinned out. The need to keep a greater distance made my pursuit more difficult, especially given the winding roads and occasional forks in them. Most of the time I was able to stay on course. Only once did I pick the wrong fork. A quick encounter with a dead end made my mistake obvious, so I quickly corrected course to get behind the pickup again.

We ended up near a cabin tucked away downhill from the road and nestled so far back among evergreens and birch trees I could barely tell the building was there. There was a gravel driveway but I stayed away from it to avoid the inevitable noisy crunching of my tires and to maintain my distance. The pickup drew up in front of the cabin and the driver went inside. I looked around for a good place to leave my car. The hilly topography gave me few options, but I managed to find the world's tiniest pull-off area and squeezed the Fiesta into it. From there, I walked back to the driveway and tried not to overly disturb the gravel as I made my way down toward the cabin.

The place apparently had no official address, that is, no house number. Not surprising, under the circumstances.

I knocked on the door, stepping to one side just in case. No shots were fired, but my spidey-sense tingled. I was being watched.

"I'm not here to hurt you," I announced. "We just need to settle a few things."

A prolonged silence followed. Then a man's voice emanated from within the mini-house. "Why? Who are you?"

"A friend. Someone who's tired of being hounded because of my work for an ingrate client."

That gave him something to think about. "Why should we talk to you?"

We? The use of the plural answered one question. "Because if you help me, I can help you, Mr. Kandinsky."

CHAPTER FORTY-FOUR

The door eased open and young Kandinsky peered through the gap.

"Who are you?" he said.

"I'm Erica Jensen. I was working for Melissa's father, but I have nothing to do with him anymore."

He squinted. "Why should I believe you?"

"Believe this," I said, holding up the death record with Melissa's name on it. "I was hired for two reasons: to find Melissa and some money your father allegedly stole from the company he co-owned with Melissa's father. At least that's what Stuart Blaine told me.

"But what really happened was your father was stealing from the Mob. And you told him you wanted no part of that. Am I right?"

As I spoke, the squinty eyes suddenly opened wide. He glanced over my shoulder. "Maybe you'd better come in."

With that, he turned and walked inside, leaving the door ajar. I pushed through and closed it behind me. Before me was a small, but comfortably furnished living area. Across the room, I spied a closed door that could have led to a bedroom or bathroom. A kitchenette was tucked into a far corner. Nice digs for a hideout.

Kandinsky slunk toward a cushiony sofa and dropped onto it. From his look, you'd have thought I'd come from the IRS to audit him.

I took a seat in a comfy-looking chair. "Before we go any further, what is your first name?"

He looked at me with suspicion all over his face.

"Come on," I said. "It's not a trick question."

The look softened. "David," he answered. The challenging edge had left his voice.

"Take my advice, David," I said. "Don't take up poker. And consider leaving the country."

He scowled. "I have nothing to worry about."

"Is that because you made a deal to split the money your dad stole? With the people he stole it from?"

"That's ridiculous." David shifted in his seat so much, he could have been doing the hula.

"Who arranged for that sniper to take a shot at me?" I asked.

"I have no idea."

Not even a hint of surprise or shock in his expression.

I rose and stood over him. "Were you trying to kill me, David? Or was it the Mob?"

He refused to look me in the eye.

"Must I kick your ass for answers?" I pressed on. A total bluff, but enough to make David squirm even more.

"No one wanted to kill anyone," he said. "But when my father was murdered, I knew he'd done something to piss off his so-called business associates. They let me keep some of the stolen money, in exchange for keeping clear of them. The sniper and the photo of your friend . . . they were warnings. They wanted you to stop looking into everything. I wanted you to stop."

"And that's it, huh?" I said. "No hard feelings? No more attempts on my life—fake or otherwise?"

"Right." David looked contrite. "Just leave us alone."

There it was again. Us. "Where's Melissa?"

David gawked at me. "She's dead. You have her death record."

I leaned toward him. "Bought and paid for with mob money. I checked with the Broward County morgue. Their records show a Jane Doe processed around this date, but nothing about Melissa. I assume it didn't take much to buy this forgery."

David sat up. He went round-eyed on me again.

"The feds aren't going to stop looking for that money," I continued. "The money you and Melissa took, because she wasn't willing to wait for her trust fund. Right?"

He slumped and rubbed his face.

I heard a door open and turned toward the sound. Melissa stood in the entrance to the other room. She looked neither surprised nor angry, just tired.

CHAPTER FORTY-FIVE

Melissa's gaze locked onto mine. "Leave him alone. He's just trying to protect me."

I scrutinized her. "From what?"

She looked incredulous. "Have you met my father?" Her expression suggested a stench had enveloped her.

"Point taken. He's not the easiest guy to like."

"Ha!" She approached me, still wearing a look of disgust. "You don't know the half of it."

I held up a hand. "And I don't want to know. Just know this. The feds are looking for the money you're using to do your disappearing act. At some point, unless you leave their jurisdiction, they'll probably find you. I did."

Melissa's expression morphed from disgust to mild gratitude. "I guess I owe you."

I stood. "In that case, do me a favor. Forget that I was here. I'm done with your father and his father." I cocked my head toward David Kandinsky.

"Sure," Melissa said. She did me the huge favor of not feigning ignorance about what I meant.

"Great. By the way, I have no idea where you are or where you're going, and I plan to leave it that way." I turned to go.

My hand was on the knob when Melissa called out, "Thank you."

"Good luck." I opened the door and left.

φφφ

By the time I reached the Virginia state line, Nick had texted me twice. I was anxious to get home, and I don't text while driving. But when he pinged me a third time, I pulled into a rest area to reply.

Each message asked how I was doing. By the third message, something in his words, "please get back to me ASAP" hinted at panic.

I sent back "I'm fine. Mission accomplished. Coming home now." I resisted the urge to add, "I had no idea you cared so much." Smiley-face.

CHAPTER FORTY-SIX

Three weeks later, I was in the midst of a routine due diligence check on a potential employee. Not for me, but for an actual small client I'd managed to scrounge up through Nick's connections. My new client was thoroughly legit and (as far as I knew) had no underworld contacts. Maybe I could manage to run my own business without having to fear for my life. Now I was glad to have met Nick the way I did. Who knew that I'd actually get a benefit out of going to those damn group therapy sessions?

When I heard the knock at my door, I rose and checked through the peephole. Maybe it was Fed Ex. Or not.

Turned out to be my pal from the FBI. Well, well.

Might as well rip this band aid off here and now. I opened up.

"Agent Phipps," I said. "What brings you here?"

"Just need to clarify a few things, Ms. Jensen," Phipps replied. Looked like I wasn't the only investigator who preferred the element of surprise to phoning ahead. We exchanged a few more bullshit pleasantries before Phipps got to the point.

"I've been trying to reach you," Phipps said. "But you don't answer your phone."

"You could have left a message."

Phipps cocked his head. "I hope you'll consider putting my number in your contacts. You still have my card?"

"Of course. At the risk of sounding defensive, why would I put an FBI agent's number in my phone?"

Phipps shared the ghost of a smile. "We could help each other."

Enough already. "What do you want from me?" I said.

"Any information you have about David Kandinsky or Stuart Blaine's daughter."

I shrugged. "Well, if that's all you need, hang on."

Leaving Phipps at the door, I retrieved the death certificate I'd been waving about like a flag.

Phipps looked the document over. He raised an eyebrow. "Is this all you have?"

"What more do you want? A treasure map?"

The ghost smile returned. "Is this your only copy?"

"Keep it," I said. "My treat."

Phipps nodded once. "Don't forget. I have friends in law enforcement. If you ever need a reference."

"Thanks," I said. "Good luck with . . . whatever."

I closed the door. Phipps' words lingered. Were they a promise or a threat?

ACKNOWLEDGMENTS

Before I start thanking everyone, I'd like to mention that Erica is a brand new protagonist, which required me to learn a whole lot about women in the military and life after discharge.

I am eternally grateful to all of the authors, editors, agents, publishers, critics, readers, librarians, booksellers, and the rest of you who inspired and advised me along the way. But special thanks are due to the members of my writers group: Mary Ellen Hughes, Becky Hutchison, Sherriel Mattingly, Bonnie Settle, Marcia Talley, and Cathy Wiley. And heartfelt thanks go out to Sisters in Crime and its Chesapeake Chapter. One of the best resources for crime writers, regardless of gender.

To acquaint myself with the life of a female Marine, I read several books by or about female Marines and soldiers—two different things. I learned that you never call a Marine a soldier. And there's no such thing as an ex-Marine, unless you get kicked out of the Corps. In disgrace.

To write authentically about post-traumatic stress, opioid addiction, and Maryland law regarding the licensing of private investigators, I was fortunate to be mentored by numerous experts, including Master Trooper George Brantley of the Maryland State Police, as well as various psychologists, journalists, private eyes, other writers, and Marines. Any errors are my own.

Finally, I'd be remiss if I failed to acknowledge the small team of freelancers who are indispensable when it comes to publishing a book. They include my editor, John Barclay-Morton, publications specialist Laurie Cullen, and graphic artist Stewart A. Williams (with an assist from Eric Ward) who designed the cover. Most of all, I thank my family and my husband who did more than they will ever know to help make this book possible.

ABOUT THE AUTHOR

Debbi Mack is the New York Times bestselling author of the Sam McRae mystery series. She has also published a young adult novel, *Invisible Me*, and a thriller, *The Planck Factor*. Debbi has also had several short stories published in various anthologies and has been nominated for a Derringer Award. She has recently become a podcaster and screenwriter who also happens to blog.

A former attorney, Debbi has also worked as a journalist, reference librarian, and freelance writer/researcher. She enjoys reading, movies, long walks, dreaming up new story lines, cats, espresso, travel, more cats, chocolate, and wondering when the fun will end.

And surprising people.

www.debbimack.com

CPSIA information can be obtained
at www.ICGtesting.com
Printed in the USA
LVHW091733110521
687112LV00007B/1116